MORE *BETTER* DEALS

JOE R. LANSDALE

MULHOLLAND
BOOKS
HODDER

First published in Great Britain in 2020 by Mulholland Books
An Imprint of Hodder & Stoughton
An Hachette UK company

This paperback edition published in 2021

1

A CIP catalogue record for this title is available from the British Library

Paperback ISBN 978 1 473 67813 2

Printed and bound in Great Britain by Clays Ltd, Elcograf S.p.A.

Hodder & Stoughton policy is to use papers that are natural, renewable
and recyclable products and made from wood grown in sustainable forests.
The logging and manufacturing processes are expected to conform to the
environmental regulations of the country of origin.

Hodder & Stoughton Ltd
Carmelite House
50 Victoria Embankment
London EC4Y 0DZ

www.hodder.co.uk

For Chet Williamson and Laurie Williamson.
Friends

He who is not contented with what he has, would not be contented with what he would like to have.

Socrates

MORE *BETTER* DEALS

(1)

I folded the check and put it in my shirt pocket and tried not to grin. The husband, a Mr. Diedre, had just bought a used Buick that had been on the lot awhile, and his wife, a cute little thing in pink chiffon and goofy white ruffles, looked like she was happy enough to keep the hubby busy all night long and not be sad about it.

The Buick they bought wasn't but a couple years old, a '62 model, but it had been driven hard and an insane number of miles were racked up on it. The owner, a seventeen-year-old, had a heavy foot. His parents took the car from him and made him get a sacking job at the Piggly Wiggly.

I knew how hard and how much the car had been driven because I had rolled back the odometer, bringing it down to a number so low I could say the car had belonged to a little old lady who bought it to drive to church on Sundays and the grocery store on Mondays; and died suddenly and her son traded it in because he didn't know what else to do with it. Simple story. Simple lie.

I had the car's transmission worked on a little, but within a few days, if the couple made a hard hill more than once or decided to get in any kind of hurry, that transmission would drop like a turd,

1

if the radiator didn't go first. It had a small hole in it that I had plugged, but that plug was like chewing gum stuck in a hole in Hoover Dam. It wasn't going to hold. It was mostly there on its honor, and it wasn't a vow it could maintain. But to make up for all that, the car was overpriced and the tires weren't as good as they looked.

By the time they figured out they owned a turnip that would cost more to fix than what they'd paid for it, it would be too late. Way Smiling Dave worked, him being the fellow owned the business, was any car paid for, once you drove it off the lot, was all yours, and so were any problems that came with it.

We cashed checks pretty quick.

Diedre might come back angry, but there wasn't much he could do about it. The rule was on our little black-and-white signs. We had them all over the place and they said all deals were final. The signs were many, but small, and the lettering was even smaller. That way we didn't make people nervous right off. It was also in our contracts, but few people actually read them, and even if they did, they wanted a car and had the money, they bought it. A bought car was purchased and made it onto the street, you were done, and so were we.

On top of that I had been known to knock a disgruntled head or two, and Smiling Dave, about two hundred and fifty pounds of lard on a five-foot-five frame mounted on tiny feet, had a cheap pistol in the desk drawer in his office, which was also my office.

I had a smaller desk and a less comfortable chair. I could look at him and see him coughing over his cigar, hear him wheezing wind, squeaking around in his swivel chair. Place always smelled like someone had set fire to a tobacco barn. I don't smoke myself. Nasty habit. Winds you and burns holes in your clothes, makes you smell the way the office smells. I can't handle a woman that smokes. I like to kiss one that doesn't taste like an ashtray or yesterday's chewing tobacco.

I came into the office and gave the Diedre check to Smiling Dave and told him he might want to take it to the bank.

He pursed his lips, studied the contract and the check. "Got yourself a nice commission there, Ed. You done all right. What is that, three cars this week?"

"Yeah. And one of them might even last out the year. I got to get home a little early today. Got a dog to kick and an old lady to push down the stairs."

"Don't grow a conscience, Ed. It's bad for your bank account. You know what they say. Buyer beware, and better you fucked than me."

I went over and sat in my little chair behind my little desk and squinted against the cigar smoke.

Smiling Dave squeaked his chair in my direction, put his cigar in a big clay ashtray his kid made for him at camp. It looked like a hunk of mud someone had beat an indention into with their fist. DAD was scratched into the side of it as if by an arthritic hand.

"I got something I need you to do. Repossess that red Caddy I sold a while back to a couple named Craig."

"That one was damn near a new car."

"Yep, and in good shape. Not our usual bucket of nuts and bolts and our best wishes. I didn't try and have them buy it outright, too expensive, and worth it for a change. I let them pay on it, couple that bought it. Only way I could sell that one for what it was worth. Not many folks going to walk in here with the kind of money to buy a barely used Caddy."

"So what did the woman look like?"

"You know me, that's for sure. I wouldn't kick her out of bed for eating crackers."

"Figured as much, you making a deal like that."

3

"Hey, I got to look at her legs, got the down payment and two months of payments, then they stopped paying. Tried calling them, sent a letter. No response."

"You try carrier pigeon?"

"That would be you, Ed. You're my carrier pigeon. Might want to take that blackjack you got, maybe some brass knuckles. Her husband is a pretty big guy. Doesn't look like he could flip over a truck with his bare hands every day, but he looks like he could hit a guy in the eye and loosen some teeth."

"All right, I'll get over there after work."

"No need to do that. Go during work hours, you want. Hell, I'm not paying you enough for after-hours work."

"You're not paying much for regular hours either. A few dollars and commission."

"Shit, Ed. You sell a lot of cars. You get a good commission. You aren't having to punch the clock and wear a tie. You got those sports coats and tassels on your shoes. Which look silly, by the way."

"This from a fat man with cigar ash on his shirt."

Smiling Dave chuckled. "Yeah, but I got my personality to fall back on."

(2)

It was late afternoon after work, and I had a cup of coffee and listened to the radio at the apartment, then I got the papers together I might need and decided to drive out to repossess the Cadillac.

First, I called my sister and told her I would pick her up, and she could drive my car back for me.

"Because I'm at your beck and call," Melinda said.

"No. Because I'll pay you ten dollars."

"Now we're talking."

When I got to the trailer park lot where Melinda lived, she was sitting on the steps reading a magazine. It was hard for me to imagine she was nineteen now. She had turned into a smart and pretty woman, and the idea of her spending her time working at the aluminum-chair factory irked me, but then again, I wasn't exactly a role model. She saw me drive up, left the magazine on the steps, and got in the car, her long black hair bouncing on her shoulders.

"Hello, brother dear."

"What the hell is that you're wearing?"

"They call them shorts in a lot of places."

"Well, they're short."

"You like women who show their legs."

"Yeah, but they aren't my little sister."

"Before we go, want to come in and see Mother?"

"Not just now," I said.

The address on the contract put the Craigs outside of town. They had a large chunk of property with a drive-in theater on it, THE HIGH-TONE DRIVE-IN, and next to it was a fenced-in slice of land, maybe five acres or more, that had a metal sign above the entrance that said PET HEAVEN. All around it was a classy split-rail fence. That seemed like an odd choice for a cemetery of any kind, but that's how it was done. There were a lot of graves out there, and nearby a couple of buildings, both pretty large, and one of them was larger than the other and looked like it might be a garage.

There were a lot of trees at the edge of the cemetery, and there was a little road that wound down behind them. The house sat close to the road and there was a gravel drive that led up to it. The house was a little white job that needed a new roof and someone to cut the grass. It had a white picket fence around it, and a white slat-board gate, and a flagstone walkway.

I didn't see the Caddy, hoped it was in the garage.

I parked in front of the gate.

Melinda said, "Not a bad house, and you say they got the grave-yard and the picture show?"

"Yeah."

"You'd think two businesses, they could make a car payment."

"You got to have a pet to bury before they get any cemetery money, but the drive-in, maybe. Lot of teenagers go."

"Yeah, me and Jody go sometimes so we can fool around."

"Don't tell me anymore about it, sis. Leaving the keys in the car, just in case you need to go quick. Sometimes people get rowdy. Slide over behind the wheel when I get out."

I leaned across Melinda and got the blackjack out of the glove box and dropped it in my coat pocket.

"Damn, Ed. You going to beat a payment out of them?"

"Just making sure the conversation stays on an even keel."

I got out, unlatched the gate and walked up the rock-slab walk to the front door.

I knocked and tried to not look threatening. A woman answered the door, pushed the screen wide, making me step back. I stepped slightly forward when the screen was pressed open, let my body hold it that way. The woman blocked the doorway by leaning on the door frame.

Mrs. Craig, I presumed. She looked about twenty-five or so. She was holding a tall drinking glass with flower designs on it, and the glass was nearly full of a pink liquid that made me think of blood in the water. She was blond in a cheap out-of-the-bottle way, had arched eyebrows and lips that could talk a man into anything, maybe some women. She wasn't wearing any makeup. She didn't need it. She was barefoot with long, brown legs in snow-white short-shorts so tight you couldn't have slipped a shoe spoon into them, and there was more nice business in a tight blue blouse that had a kind of pull tie across her belly. I could see her navel. It was a nice navel. I'd have licked champagne or chocolate out of that navel. Fact was, I might have licked pond water out of it if that's what she had in it.

Her eyes were kind of narrow, and I'd say that was her only flaw, way those black eyes looked at me standing there, like an alligator that was about to bite my head and roll with me down into deep water from which there would be no coming up.

I found my hand drifting into my coat for the blackjack. I can't rightly explain that, but I remember that and thinking, It's just a woman, a fine-looking one, and a blackjack probably won't be necessary.

7

"Mrs. Craig," I said.

"That's me."

"Is your husband home?"

"Nope. You figure I can't do business unless he's here?"

"I'm here on a matter that might require both of you present."

"Nice save, big guy."

"May I come in?"

"You come here, smile at me, and you think that's going to move me to let you in?"

"I certainly hoped it would."

"You through looking at my legs?"

"Not as long as they're there to look at."

She smirked and sipped her drink. She studied me the way a shopper studies fish at the fish market. "You look like someone mixed you up with the right ingredients, handsome."

"Oh, I don't know. I think maybe there's too much salt."

She smiled then. She had movie-star teeth. "Who's that in the car, your girlfriend or your getaway driver?"

I looked back and saw Melinda had slid behind the wheel as I'd asked. She gave me a little wave.

"My sister. She's waiting on me, but no rush."

"Come in," she said.

She walked back into the house, and I slipped in after her, careful not to let the screen door slam.

There was a big swamp cooler in the living-room window. We went past the living room, that cooler ruffling our hair, and into the kitchen. The back door was open, but the screen was shut. It was growing dusky outside, but I could see the cemetery from there, and the two buildings out back, and between them a clearing full of tall grass and the woods beyond.

There was a big pitcher on the table full of a reddish liquid and ice cubes were floating in it. Around the table were cheap chairs with blue plastic backs. There were rubber place mats, and one of them had a water ring that I knew would fit the bottom of her glass.

She sat down and didn't offer me a chair. I pulled one out and sat down, pulled the folded papers I had with me, the ones concerning the Cadillac, out of my sports-coat pocket and placed them in front of me and smoothed them out on the table.

She said, "Something to drink?"

I didn't know what was in the pitcher, but it looked cold, and though the swamp cooler was straining, about the only thing it was doing was making the air feel damp. It wasn't any better than rubbing your face with a warm, wet towel.

"Sure," I said. I knew I should have just gotten it over with, but something about her kept me stalling. She didn't seem to be in any hurry to find anything out, so what was my rush?

She got up and pulled a glass out of the cabinet and brought it back to me. Way she moved was like a sex ballet. She placed the glass on the table, poured some of the liquid from the pitcher into it, and sat it in front of me on the rubber mat and partly on the contract.

I moved the glass as she sat down. I took a sip from the glass. It was some kind of strawberry drink, and it had enough whiskey in it to pickle an eel.

"Well, that's certainly an evening bracer," I said.

"Yeah, I thought I'd have a glass or two of it before dinner, then skip dinner."

"I suppose I should get right down to business."

"Suit yourself."

"It's about the Cadillac."

"You mean the one that hasn't been paid on?"

"Exactly."

"Yeah. Well, I got a beat-up old jalopy in the outbuilding out there, but no Cadillac."

"Well, you bought a Cadillac."

"My husband did, and he's not here. He's in it, or maybe he's out of it and drinking somewhere, might be fucking or fighting. Maybe both at the same time. I don't even know where he is. He hasn't been around in two months or so. He took the Caddy and quit payments. Another couple of weeks, more bills are coming due. I might have to get a job if I don't start hooking first. That's a joke, by the way."

"I see. So he's got the car?"

"I'm pretty sure I said that."

"Suppose you did. Being as the payments are due, we need either the money or the car. You can pay me today."

"No, I can't. I haven't got the money."

"When's your husband coming back?"

"Can't say. Don't know. But if he comes back, he likes a Monday. Rarely comes back on a Tuesday, but the rest of the days are a toss-up."

"Where's he work?"

"Traveling salesman."

"Selling what?"

"Encyclopedias."

"Come on."

"Seriously. Listen . . . what's your name?"

"Edwards."

"What Edwards?"

"Ed Edwards."

"Damn. Is your middle name Ed too?"

"Thing is, Mrs. Craig——"

"Nancy."

"The bill is overdue and we have to either get our money or repossess it. I'm sorry, that's just how it works. You buy something, you have to pay for it."

"Let me put it like this. What I said before about money, not having any, nothing has changed since I mentioned that unless a rich uncle died somewhere and left me something. Maybe later I'll get a telegram. As for the car, you can take it for all I care, but the thing is I don't have it. You find my husband, Frank, you take it from him. Which, by the way, might require some strenuous effort. He's what you might call rambunctious."

"All right, then," I said. "I guess I'll go."

"Drink your drink."

I took another sip of it, felt my liver try to hide behind a lung, and put the glass down. "That'll do me," I said.

I got up and made a production of pushing my chair under the table and picking up the contract. I shook it a little. "You signed a contract."

"Nope. Frank did."

"I'll be back."

"Lose the sports coat. Dress up next time. Maybe we'll go dancing. Frank's home, we can drive somewhere in the Cadillac. But I get the feeling you're more of a Dairy Queen guy and you like to drink at home with a TV dinner."

"Sometimes I have my beer and TV dinner with someone," I said.

"So you have a dog?"

"Goodbye, Mrs. Craig. Until next time, when I take the car."

"Frank's home, you might want to bring a tire iron."

I thought about the blackjack in my coat pocket. I figured that would be enough.

(3)

had Melinda slide over and I slipped in behind the wheel. It had grown solid dark by that time.

"Well?" Melinda said.

"She says she doesn't know where the car is. That her husband has it, and he hasn't been around in a couple months, sells encyclopedias on the road."

"You believe that?"

"Nope. Well, he might not be around and he might sell encyclopedias, but I got this hunch the car is out there in the garage."

"So I still get the ten dollars?"

"You do. Use it to buy some pants, a dress, maybe."

"You could give that woman a ten, have her buy some pants."

"Well, once again, she's not my sister."

"She doesn't look like someone could be anyone's sister."

I dropped Melinda off with a ten in her hand, went home, put a TV dinner in the oven, and got a beer out of the refrigerator. I sat at the kitchen table and drank the beer and watched the stove like I was waiting on the Resurrection.

When the dinner was done, I put it on the little table in front of the couch, turned on the TV, got myself another beer and a fork, came back, and flopped my ass down.

Nancy had figured me pretty close. Beer and a TV dinner, but no dog.

I ate the dinner, watched a little TV, mostly cowboys shooting people off horses, and then I turned it off and read awhile. I had three days of newspapers backed up.

When I finished reading them, I realized I could have just as well not read them. There wasn't anything in them that stuck to me. Right then, maybe nothing would stick to me.

I kept thinking about Nancy and her long legs and that tight blouse and that belly button, and I kept thinking too she seemed excessively world-weary for someone that young. But I was young and felt that way myself. The Korean War will do that to a fella. I wondered what Nancy's husband was like. I didn't get the feeling she missed him being gone. I wondered if maybe he was actually around. He might have been in the back room, for all I knew, had let her talk to me and soften me up.

I got the contract and looked it over. She was closer to my age than I expected. Her maiden name was Woodward, and she was from a little town called Gladewater. She had a ninth-grade education and a Baptist raising, as she had written that in where it asked for her religion. She didn't seem like a devoted churchgoer to me.

Her husband's name was Frank. He was thirty-six. In the religion slot, he wrote *None*. Well, me and him had that in common. For occupation, he wrote in *sales*. Also a connection.

Maybe Nancy hadn't lied. Maybe he was on the road, and when he got back, he would make a nice juicy payment and fill in the ones he missed.

And maybe not.

I got my coat with the blackjack in the pocket, put it on, and drove back out to the Craig place. I didn't park in front of the gate this time. I parked down from the pet cemetery, off the little road that was bordered by trees. I kind of liked that idea. I once had a dog and he was buried in an abandoned yard, and now and again I still thought about him. I thought about a lot of things, none of them particularly important.

I could see the lights from the drive-in, and I could see a bit of the screen from where I stood. There was a monster movie on. I loved a good monster movie, but tonight I wouldn't be seeing one.

I walked over to the cemetery, slipped through the split-rail fence that went around it, mostly as decoration, and started walking toward the buildings behind the house. Nancy said she had an old heap parked there, but I wanted to make sure it didn't have a ritzy companion by the name of Cadillac.

It wasn't a bright night, but the lights from the drive-in made it so I could be seen if someone was looking. I glanced toward the house, but there was only one light in a window. A back room.

I took out my little penlight and used it to flash around the cemetery. There were a few headstones, but there were mostly metal markers that had the shape of an animal at the top, dog or cat, though there was one that was either a parakeet or a parrot.

I paused at a marker that said BENNY, HE WAS A GOOD HORSE. Under that, someone had scratched in *But he should have watched for cars.*

I made my way through the fence on the other side and over to the bigger building, a kind of metal barn, one I thought would serve as a garage, and checked to see if the wide doors in the front were locked. They weren't.

I pushed one of them back and went inside, pulled the door closed behind me. There was a jalopy there, all right, but there was also a nice little Cadillac, the one that had come from our lot. There was a little motorboat in front of the cars, a lawn mower. Tools hanging on the walls.

I opened the Caddy door, and the interior light came on. I looked to see if she kept the keys in the ignition. She didn't. I checked behind the sun visor. Nope.

I would have to hot-wire it. I was pretty good at that. While I was under the dash, maybe I could roll back the odometer, just to have it done for the next owner, who in this case would actually get a good deal. I liked the car myself. I thought I'd look good driving it around. I got it back to the lot, I'd call and wake up Melinda, have her pick me up, bring me back to pick up my car.

I was about to slide in and go to work with my pocketknife on the wires under the dash when I heard the barn door open. I pulled my head out of the car and saw Nancy outlined in the open doorway.

She had on a short black dress and was wearing high heels and holding what looked like a cannon in her hand.

(4)

It wasn't actually a cannon, but it was a twelve-gauge. I recognized it. I had inherited one from my dad that was just like it. Except, of course, mine was home and in the hall closet. I hadn't thought I'd need it. The blackjack was about as handy right then as an extra thumb. I put my hands up without being asked.

"You here to check the air in the tires?"

"I was afraid, long as you've had it, tires might need some inflation, and we at Smiling Dave's are here to serve."

"Always more better deals and service with a smile."

"You nailed it."

"Obviously, I lied to you."

"Obviously. I see the car here, I got to wonder how your husband sells encyclopedias. He ride a stick horse and carry all those books on his back?"

"He works in tandem with a friend. The friend owns the car they're using this time out. And he only carries samples, not the whole set of encyclopedias, smart-ass."

"Since I'm here, why don't you let me drive the car around the block as a courtesy?"

"You're trying awfully hard to be funny."

"The gun makes me nervous. I get goofy when I'm scared."

"You get scared a lot?"

"I don't get guns pointed at me a lot, but my guess is that'll always do that. Scare me, I mean. May I put my hands down?"

"Go ahead, just don't put them in your pockets, case you got a gun on you."

"I didn't figure I'd have to shoot the car. I thought it would go peacefully. You always get dressed up to hunt down repo men?"

She lowered the shotgun. "I was going out to the fucking Piggly Wiggly."

"No, you weren't."

"You're right. I was going to a honky-tonk. But I'm flexible. Want to come up to the house for a nightcap, and maybe we could roll around on the bed and screw?"

"Do we have to have the nightcap?"

(5)

We skipped the nightcap. We went up to the house and she put the shotgun away and took off her dress and, I guess because she thought it might excite me, left on the high heels.

I didn't end up needing the blackjack, though once or twice it was something I considered, just to tire her out a little. What she didn't know was, screw her or not, I was going to take the Cadillac.

We lay there in bed, my arm around her shoulders, her hand under the covers, cupping my balls. There was a fan in the bedroom window, and it was pretty cool for a change.

"That really your sister in the car earlier, not a girlfriend?"

"Yep."

"You Puerto Rican?"

"No. Why do you ask?"

"You, and what I could see of her, look a little that way. It's okay with me, I'm just asking."

"No. Not Puerto Rican. You Irish?"

"Maybe. I think a little."

"Shit. I don't fuck Irish."

She squeezed my balls enough to make me flinch. "I got you by the balls, buster. You better play nice."

"I withdraw the question and deny it. Personally, I sing 'Danny Boy' every morning before work and have some shamrocks flattened inside some books."

"What kind of books? Comic books?"

"All kinds of books. So, the husband. Does he have a shotgun too?"

"I don't think so, but he might have something."

"He's not going to come in here and take photos of you holding my nuts and blackmail me to keep the Cadillac, is he?"

"The lights are out, silly. And my hand is under the covers. He's going to come out of the closet later, when I turn the lights on and give you a blow job."

"I got to warn you, I don't care if photos get around of that. Women, even men, they get just a glance of what I got, no one will ever satisfy them again."

"That right?"

"You bet."

"You're not that good, mister."

"Oh. I don't get an A plus?"

"I'll give you an A minus. You at least know I have a clit and can find it without directions."

"It's not that well hidden."

"I gave you a minus because you didn't try out doggy-style."

"Hell, lady. The night is young."

"Don't call me a lady."

(6)

After that corny business, we did some better business, and finally we were in our underwear at the table having that nightcap, this time without the strawberry drink and the water.

From the window, I could see the drive-in and the big lighted sign that ran straight up on a rack. It was covered in golden lights and looked like a giant finger pointing to the heavens. There was something warm and inviting about it. In the day, it was just cold, dead bulbs in a pattern, but at night, those lights lit up spelled out HIGH-TONE DRIVE-IN. It gave me a kind of sweet chill to see those lights. There was a magic about them, and I wanted to be part of that magic.

She slugged back two drinks before I finished the one, and when she tried to pour me another, I put my hand over the top of the glass.

"I don't know where you buy your whiskey, but that's some stuff right there, and I think I've had enough."

"Me and Frank sometimes drink a whole bottle at night."

"But he's not here to drink it."

"Rarely is here."

"Drive-in run without you?"

"I got a manager. I think he skims on me, but at least that gives me a night off now and then. There're days when I've smelled enough popcorn, dealt with enough high-school boys with zits and hard-ons, and had enough of monster movies. I have to have time to myself, so I count the skimming as overtime pay."

"That's no way to run a business."

"You think you could run it better?"

"Better than that."

"Maybe I had someone around I liked having around, I could do better myself."

"You do okay with the pet cemetery?"

"I hate that. Me and Frank bought this place, the land, it was from an old lady who had established the cemetery. She was so loony she could hear birds singing in a well. But we bought the place, and most of the people who have pets out there, or think they do, they pay to keep up the cemetery, which amounts to pulling a few weeds and mowing the grass between graves.

"I saw vandals have been at it. Ben the horse has a little epigram carved on its headstone. Little girl whose pet it was wrote that with a nail file. Her daddy turned a corner around some trees, and—surprise—the pet horse had gotten out and was within moments a hood ornament. The girl, I guess maybe she's six."

"And has a nail file?"

"Probably high heels and a box of rubbers too. They start trying to be women early these days."

"You embalm the pets?"

"That's what the other building is for. Lady we bought it from, she was getting too old to do the business. She showed us how to prepare the animals for their final rest, but it's tedious. Be honest with you, Ed, what we found out is digging a hole is work. So we mound the dirt up a little, scrape some here or there and make it look like a grave, then we take the beloved off in the woods and throw it in a ditch somewhere. We have a ceremony they want it. Sometimes they don't. Usually it's kids come out to visit their pet's grave—that is, until they get a new pet or hit puberty and lose interest in a dead dog. Way it works, pet owner's happy, and we get paid and we're not wearing out our backs.

"Pony was an exception. I think we lost money on that one. It was too big to load up and drop in the woods. We had to hire a wrecker, a goddamn wrecker, to load that horse up and bring it out here, and then we had a crate made because the owner had some money and wanted it that way and came out to check. We actually had to embalm it, rent a backhoe to dig the grave, then hire about twelve people to help us lower it in. Had a big service. All the little rich girl's friends came out dressed up like they were going to Easter Sunday, and they had a preacher give a sermon and say some words. Much money as they spent, we still lost money on that one, the wrecker, backhoe, and all. I made a rule right then: No more dead ponies."

"That's discouraging. I have a pet elephant, and lately he hasn't been looking so good."

"I like you. I like a man tries to be funny, even if he isn't. I like to know he's got a sense of humor, even when it isn't a good one."

"Let me tell you something else funny. I'm going to need the keys to the Cadillac."

"You son of a bitch. You come up here and try to steal my car, and then you steal my pussy, and now you want the car keys to just drive it off."

"Technically, I'm not stealing anything. Car or pussy. You don't own the car, and the pussy came with a nightcap."

"Don't be vulgar."

"I'm just talking how you're talking. Look here, I don't want to sideline you on the Cadillac, but I don't take it, some professional repo men will be hired, and they'll take it anyway. I'm actually trying to help you out here."

"That's funny, I thought just the opposite."

"Here's the thing. You give me the keys, and I'm going to buy the car myself, pay it out in payments. That way we don't have to make a legal matter out of it. I just take the car. I'm thinking you could have paid if Frank would have let you, so I don't see you at fault." I didn't really think that, but it sounded good. I had a feeling Nancy would steal a nickel if someone offered to give it to her.

"Frank is tight with money. He likes to buy things and pay only so much, then he quits. I've had some appliances come in and go out like they were just here for a visit. I was happy to get the swamp cooler paid off. It gets hot this time of year."

"That's the deal I can make you," I said. "I think it's a good one. I can come pick you up and take you out, and you got the jalopy to drive around town. Bring it by the lot, maybe I can trade it in for something a step up, though considering the step you're on, all I can guarantee is it'll be a little better. I bet I can get you one for free."

"Yeah?"

"Sure, but again, it won't be top of the line. Think of it like going from a leg that's a stump to getting a peg for it."

"That doesn't sound like that good a deal."

"It's the deal I got."

"You're either the best con man I've ever met, and I pride myself on certain skills, or you're the dumbest son of a bitch ever squatted to shit over a pair of shoes."

"I'll accept either moniker."

She sat there in her underwear awhile, and I sat there in mine. She had another drink. I poured myself a short one. We had the back door open and there was only the door screen, but with the light on in the kitchen, insects were gathering on it, and the air coming through, even without the bedroom fan or the swamp cooler, was pretty pleasant. Neither of us was in a hurry.

"All right," she said.

(7)

I had the Cadillac and was buying it as planned, made a deal with Smiling Dave to trade in the one I had. I didn't tell him all that Nancy had told me about her business, but I did tell him I wanted to take up payments minus what she and Frank had paid, and he let me.

He should have. So far that week, I'd sold three cars, and I came in on Saturday, my day off, and sold another. I didn't plan on actually letting Nancy have the car in the end either. Never trust a used-car salesman. I also didn't plan on seeing her again, but I won't lie to you, I thought about her. Her long legs and that blond hair and that belly button. I thought about that drive-in theater and the cemetery that only had a dead horse in it and some scraped-up dirt and some markers with nothing under them, their planned-for occupants out in the woods somewhere rotting away. That seemed like a nice combination of businesses.

"What did you think about that Craig woman? Some looker, huh."

"She was all right."

"All right? Shit, boy, there's men that would have crawled over ten miles of broken glass naked and fought a pack of savage midgets to get some of that."

"Savage midgets?"

"It just came to mind."

"Yeah. Well, I got a close first cousin that's a midget, just a little-bitty guy, and I find that talk offensive."

"Hey, Ed. I'm sorry."

I laughed. "I'm fucking with you. He's not even a first cousin."

Dave squeaked his chair around so that he could look right at me. "Asshole. How about some coffee?"

"Sure. Which means I get up and make it."

"This body doesn't get around as good as yours. And besides, I'm the boss."

I stood up, got the percolator set up and the Folgers in it, put it on the hot plate, and got it going. I took two cups out of the overhead pantry and set them beside the hot plate, sat down, and waited. We talked some more about this and that, then we drank coffee, and Smiling Dave smoked a turd rope.

"You know, Ed, there's times I lie down at night, think maybe I'm pushing the line too much, selling some of the kinds of junk cars I sell."

"We sell some good ones too."

"Does that make it better? The now-and-then good car, like that Caddy? I lay down, think about some piece of junk I've sold someone, made money off of, and lot of them folks have families and such. I mostly get this way when I have indigestion, and a little later, after an Alka-Seltzer, I say fuck 'em, buyer beware. But I got moments when I think about some of the exaggerations—shit, lies I've told. Some of them stink so bad, I damn near think the Department of Health will show up, have me quarantined. You ever have moments like that?"

"Nope."

"Yeah. Well, used to I didn't either. I get a few now. I think it's old age. There's a sentimental element to it. Wish I didn't get that way at all."

"Take another Alka-Seltzer."

"Yeah. I hear you."

"You going to start giving fairer prices, truer deals, Dave?"

"Oh, hell no. It's just a feeling now and then, not a transition of philosophy. What we got going for us, Ed, is that people think life is fair, that it'll work out for them. That the government has their best interests at heart. That commercials on TV are trying to sell them something worth having when most of what they're selling is just to sell it. Know how to talk up a bucket of shit as a cure for baldness, there's some meathead will buy it and pour it on his slick noggin. You play on what people think is right, and what they think is some special product, then they got to have it. Everyone's got to have it. I tell someone that dead-rat smell in the trunk of a car is new-car smell, if they want the car, that's what they'll start smelling. We convince them. It might stink like a dead rat a week later, but for a few days, they're driving around in it while it's still working okay, it's a smell they like."

(8)

A couple weeks passed. Dave had gone to get a burger and bring me back one, and I was standing in the office, looking out the window, thinking things had turned a little slow, and I see Nancy driving up in her piece of junk.

Electric butterflies fluttered along my spine when I saw her and there was a vibration in my head like someone had set off a tuning fork. I went out and met her in the lot just as she was getting out of her car.

She was wearing blue jeans today, kind that looked like she had been poured into them, and a nice top and tennis shoes. Her hair was a bit wild-looking, like a palomino horse with its mane in the wind.

When she got out of the car, she gave me a look that made me step back a pace.

"You are some kind of shit, Ed."

"I'm a used-car salesman. What did you expect?"

"My dad was a used-car salesman, and honest."

"That right?"

"Yep. He hardly kept food on the table but didn't lie about the junk he sold. I got to tell you, Ed, that was some line of crap you pitched me, about coming to take me out. And I bought it. I been around for a girl my age, seen some things, but I bought it."

"When did you decide it was crap?"

"When you were telling it to me, but later I got mad about it."

"Yeah. I'm pretty good. I have time to work on my patter out here in the lot and, on slow days, in the office."

She smiled. It surprised me. "Okay, you got the Cadillac, but I been thinking about that night, and I been thinking about my husband being gone, and I been thinking you might want to come back over, have a drink, and haul my ashes, no Cadillac involved. I mean, you already got the milk, you might as well come back and visit the cow."

"I've thought about it."

"I bet you have, but you didn't come. One thing, though. You said you'd fix me up with a better car for free. Was that bullshit too?"

"Pretty much. But you want to pay a little, got the money, pay it outright, I can put you in something better than you got."

"You're a piece of work, Ed."

"And so are you."

"The fox doesn't like to get outfoxed, that's the thing."

"Tell you what. You trade in that piece of shit and let me pick you out a car that is cheap but runs well, and I'll put a new set of tires on it and buy you dinner."

"I don't go out much. Married, you see."

"I can buy some groceries, come over and cook for you."

"You cook?"

"You bet."

"All right, then. Show me the car."

(9)

I did get her a car, and I even kicked in some of my own money to make it work, but I didn't tell Dave that. I got the commission, but considering how I had helped her out, it was a substantial loss. But I still had the Cadillac.

When I was a kid, my father, gone now, run off somewhere, was one of the world's greatest human train wrecks, but he told me a thing that stuck. He used to say a Cadillac gave the impression you were living well, and people would respect you, they saw you in that kind of car. You might be living in a cardboard box wrapped in a bath towel at night, but if you owned a car like that, people thought differently about you. Thing was, of course, you had to be able to have the Cadillac. And now I had one.

As for me and Nancy, things happened fast after that.

I went out to her place on summer nights, and the days went by, and then the weeks, and about ten months in, lying in bed, I said, "So, your husband. Any idea when he's coming back?"

"He won't be coming back. You could say we are divorced without papers."

"You mean separated."

"Tomayto, tomahto."

"I keep thinking, nights I'm out here, some night I'll be sleeping and I won't wake up because he'll get that shotgun you got and splatter my head all over the sheets."

"That won't happen, Ed. Frank is dead."

"Dead?"

"Yep."

"Since when?"

"I guess we're talking shortly after we bought the Cadillac."

"Paid down on the Cadillac, he died, and you didn't tell me, lied to make me think he was around?"

"That might have been a good move, to do it like that, but no. He had an accident."

"What kind of accident?"

"The kind you have when your wife sneaks up on you from behind with a hatchet."

I felt my blood chill. "You're messing with me, right?"

"No."

"Why are you telling me this?"

"I could say you did it, that we had a thing going and you did it. You hit him with an ax and then you threatened me so I wouldn't talk."

I sat up in bed. "Whoa, baby. You just said he was dead before we met, right after you bought the Cadillac from Dave. I wasn't even on the lot when you bought it."

"I could adjust my timeline a little."

"Damn, girl."

"What happened was you were infatuated with me so you decided you'd kill him. You snuck out here, picked a hatchet out of the barn, and, let's see, I can say Frank went out there, maybe to drive the Cadillac, and you came up from behind and killed him with the hatchet. I know all this because I'll say I went out there with Frank. It was a plan you made me part of on threat of death.

31

I went out there and you killed Frank, and then we buried him in the pet cemetery, put him in the box with the dead pony."

"He's buried with the pony?"

"I thought he'd like a pony ride to hell."

"Listen, Nancy. I don't like that idea you got even a little bit."

"You're not supposed to."

"I think maybe I can explain the truth to the police. I can tell them the truth and I bet they believe me."

"Over a pretty young thing that's been bullied by a big, mean used-car salesman? Like you said, those used-car folks, they're liars from the get-go. Except my ol' dad, of course. Well, the dad I made up. My real dad was a pimp and I grew up in Fort Worth with his hand between my legs."

"Look here, Nancy. You don't have to do this. I'll give you that Cadillac, no charge."

"You're lying. You just want to get out of here, but you got to understand, that won't help you."

"No. I'm serious. I can get you the Cadillac. I can make that work, and I won't say a word to anyone."

"Ha. Got you."

"What?"

"I was messing with you. You are one big sucker, Ed. You aren't so tough, and you just thought you had a line of patter. How was that?"

I breathed a large sigh of relief. I felt as if I were melting into the mattress. I was covered in sweat. "Goddamn. You had me going, all right."

"I was getting a little bit even for what you did to me, though I don't consider us exactly even yet. I pulled a joke, you got my Cadillac. I played that out a little more, I'd have that car back. But even I couldn't be that mean. Someone else, I could have. But I really do like you, Ed."

"Yeah?"

"Oh yeah, but you aren't so slick. That was a stupid story, and you bought it. I guess, though, you might have been the kind of guy that would decide to kill me to keep me from spreading that around, and then you would be a real murderer. Isn't it funny how things might go?"

"Damn, Nancy. You got a mind that goes all over the place."

That's when I should have packed it in, but there was something about her, and I don't just mean her looks and the sweet and musky way she smelled, though that didn't hurt matters. It was something else. Something rotten and at the same time intriguing. It was like a sour kind of whiskey that you had to get used to, and because of how it made you feel, you were willing to.

Later in the night, with Nancy in a deep sleep, I went to the bathroom, and after I washed my hands, I got to thinking.

I quietly opened some bathroom cabinets and looked around. There was a shaving kit. I pulled the zipper and looked inside. Shaving cup with a bar of soap in the bottom of it, a shaving brush, and a double-edged razor and some blades.

Guy leaves, wouldn't he take his shaving kit? What was in the bedroom closet? His clothes?

Stop it, Ed, I told myself. A guy and a girl split up, doesn't mean he takes everything with him. He might buy new, or he might plan to come back and get the stuff, or maybe he decides it's easier to forget it.

He was probably on the road selling encyclopedias. He probably had a new girl, some new clothes, and a shaving kit with a fresh toothbrush and razor.

But the thing was, Nancy had planted a seed.

(10)

The seed grew slowly. It took a while to make a tree. I kept seeing Nancy, but I slept nervous, thought of hatchets and horses and husbands and deep graves. My warning bells and whistles were going off all over the place, and I could hear them, but I refused to listen.

One afternoon I was having my beer and TV dinner, and Melinda showed up. She was wearing jeans, a sweatshirt, and tennis shoes. She looked even younger than she was. After I let her in, I went back to my TV dinner, but I stopped on my way to it and turned off the TV. It was the news. It was depressing. "What's going on, kid," I said.

"I came to get you to go back with me and see Mama."

"I'm kind of worn out."

"It doesn't take that much energy to eat a shitty TV dinner."

"I don't know," I said, "I really like to work at it. I get through, that damn little tray will be shiny like a well-oiled baby's ass."

"Yeah. Well, finish it. You're going with me. Not taking no for an answer. You haven't seen her in a while, and I'm not going to sugarcoat it—she's not doing so well."

"Still drinking, I presume."

"You know she is. Not long ago, she found some of Dad's old aftershave and hair oil and drank that. She drank a bit of furniture polish before I could get it away from her. I saw her take a swig of pure rubbing alcohol once. I grabbed it and poured it out."

"Jesus."

"I finally started buying her beer. That doesn't work for her like the whiskey, but it keeps her away from the whiskey, which makes her a little crazy."

"You're not making it a damn bit better. It's all alcohol, and it's not doing her any good."

"You're drinking a beer."

"But I don't drink but now and then, and not too much. I don't have a problem with it."

"She says the same thing."

"This isn't about me. I'm not drinking aftershave and hair oil."

"If I didn't buy her anything, well, who's to say what she'd do? She'd be slipping out and walking to town, looking for liquor. She's also got this guy comes around, sells her a pint of this or that. Sometimes the liquor is clear, sometimes brown. I can't stop that from happening. I'm at work, but I found out about it. People I know know him and they told me."

"Where's she get the money for it?"

"I don't think she's buying it with money."

"Goddamn it."

"It's just because she's got it bad, Ed. Real bad."

"Run that son of a bitch off."

"In case you haven't noticed, I'm not that big, nor am I that fierce. This guy, he's good-sized. But Ed, she's got it bad right now. She doesn't look that great."

"That's why I don't visit. It's like going over to watch someone bleed out."

"Come on, Ed. Come with me."

I finished my beer and got my coat, and we left out of there, went over to the dark den of sad dreams and at least one bad liver.

(11)

I drove over to the trailer, riding behind Melinda's heap. It was a hot night and I had the Cadillac's window down, and the speed of the car and the wind coming in wasn't much help. It felt like panting dog breath and it didn't smell a lot better, as the wind had picked up a nasty aroma, like something dead was in the woods along the road.

I didn't want to use the air conditioner for some reason. I wanted to feel that hot wind. I wanted to feel and smell something real, not artificial. I can't explain that, but that's how I felt.

When we got to the trailer, Melinda parked and I pulled up close behind her and we both got out and I followed Melinda to the door.

Inside, the mobile home smelled of a few days' cooking. At some point, they had eaten fried fish. It made my stomach knot.

The light in the living room was on, and it was bright enough I could see into the little kitchen, which was without a door. I saw a pile of greasy and food-flecked dishes piled in the sink, like dead soldiers in a common grave.

I said to Melinda, "Doesn't anyone wash the dishes?"

"Be my guest. I've switched to paper plates. Wait here a minute, let me make sure she's decent."

Melinda walked down the hall and opened the bedroom door without knocking and went in. In what light was there, I saw disturbed dust motes floating.

After what seemed like a long time, Melinda came out, closed the door, and motioned me over.

There were framed photographs on either side of the hall, and though it was dark, I had seen them all before, so I knew exactly what was in every frame. There was a photo on the right side of me that had been taken when I was small, eight or nine, when we lived on a farm. I had my arm around a white goat. A big black man stood behind me and the goat. He was wearing overalls and a fedora. He had his hand on my shoulder. The other photos were even less exciting.

When I got to the door, Melinda knocked gently, said, "Ed's here."

"Oh, my baby boy, come in, come in."

I was a middle child, but still the younger of two brothers. Melinda, of course, was the baby of the family. But Mama always called me baby boy.

Melinda walked back into the living room as I turned the doorknob.

Inside the room, the air, the walls, and curtains were baked in smoke and it was hard to breathe. Mama was sitting up in bed smoking a cigarette with an ashtray on her lap. It was already full and when she poked her cigarette into it as I came in, ash and butts fell out of the tray and onto the old blanket she had pulled over her.

For someone in her state, she was still an attractive-looking woman, but she needed to be outside and she needed to comb her graying hair that only a short time ago had been as dark as a raven's wing. There was a sheen of sweat on her face, and her eyes were reminiscent of someone shell-shocked, like the way I saw eyes in Korea, like maybe mine had been back then, right before they discharged me. Still, it was easy to see why Melinda was a beauty. She had borrowed the best parts of herself from Mama.

I went and sat on the edge of the bed and leaned over and kissed her on the cheek. She smelled like the smoking car on a train.

"It's been a while. I thought any day you'd come by and see your old mama."

"You're not that old."

"Old enough. Melinda just told me you got a Cadillac."

"A red one."

"You like it?"

"Sure."

"It's good to see you doing well enough to buy a car like that on the money you make."

"It's not so bad, and it's used."

"Not new, then?"

"Hey, I was thinking you might want to set a back fire in the kitchen."

Mama sort of coughed a laugh, like it was struggling around the cigarette smoke she'd pulled inside of herself. "Jake, he says he's going to buy me a dishwasher."

"He says a lot of things."

"At least he calls me a lot. He's done the best of all of you, though the verdict is still out on Melinda. She's still young. Depends on if she marries someone with money."

"She wants to go to college."

"She can't afford it. She needs to get out of this life. Her looks, she can make it easy, she marries the right man."

"She's got smarts. She doesn't need to waste that making cookies. She can make cookies later, she wants. She can marry later, she wants. She needs to go to school."

"Why didn't you?"

"Same problem. No money. And in my case, not as smart as her. She's special."

Mama lit another cigarette and took a deep, long drag. She let the smoke out slowly and with great satisfaction. "Jake, he's done all right," she said.

"Assembly line in Detroit. I don't know, Mama. That might be all right for him, but maybe not for me, and certainly not for Melinda. Doing all right is relative."

"He's the darkest of the three of you, and he's done all right."

"He came down solid on a side, way he looks. Me and Melinda didn't. People always think I'm Puerto Rican or Mexican, sometimes Italian. They knew the truth, I wouldn't be working at the car lot. I'd be emptying wastebaskets."

"I should never have gotten involved with a nigger."

"Damn, Mama. He was our father."

"I know. I'm just being mean. I need a drink."

"No, you don't."

"You just don't understand."

"I understand it's not doing you any good or you wouldn't be in bed this early. And all those cigarettes, that can't be good for you."

"Smoke is the only thing holding me together. Listen here, baby boy. You and Melinda, you're light enough to pass. You can do better for yourself. You can do like Jacob, but you can do even better. Don't be poor. I been poor all my life, and I don't like it. I can barely send Melinda to the store, let alone pay for college. She might have to marry her way out. But you, you're smart too, baby boy. Take advantage of your whiteness. Do something other than sell used cars."

"Do you hear from Daddy?"

"Are you kidding? I don't even know where he is. I don't know anyone knows where he is. We got back together just long enough for me to get pregnant again with Melinda. He might be dead, for all I know. He might be remarried, not that we ever had formal papers back in Fort Worth, and he might have ten kids. I don't know. I don't want to know. I don't need a dark man in my life. Life is easier when you're pale."

"It didn't do you a lot of good, did it?"

Soon as I said that, I wished I hadn't. Her face pinched. She pulled on the cigarette again and eased the smoke out through her nose.

"No, it didn't do me all that much good at all. My problem is I fell in love with the wrong person, and the wrong color."

(12)

Melinda walked me out to my car. We leaned against the hood. The air was nice. Mama's trailer was the only one in the area. It wasn't much, but she at least had a couple acres to put it on, and that gave her room. You could see houses from where her mobile home was set, but you couldn't lean out the window and shake hands with your next-door neighbor.

The porch light was on, and it shone down on the steps and made them shiny.

"She has the mark of death on her," I said.

"It's not that bad."

"Saw it in Korea. It's a look they got when they were sick or wounded, and you knew it was going to get worse, and they were going to die. And if they were okay, not sick or wounded, and they had that look, then death was coming for them. It already owned them, and all death had to do then was collect."

"That's silly."

"She has that look."

"You say."

"It's illogical, but she has that look."

"If she could stay away from the booze and those cigarettes."

42

"This guy comes around and sells her the booze. Tell me where he is."

"What you going to do?"

"Talk to him."

"Oh, that will help. That's like asking a shark not to eat you."

"Tell me where I can find him."

"I got an idea, but I better ride with you. It's a hard place to find."

"How do you know the place, then?"

"I been out there."

"With who?"

"With a man."

"A black man?"

"We're half black."

"Gee, I didn't know that. Listen, you got a chance to climb up in the world, and you ought to. Stay away from colored people, hear me?"

"You mean pass."

"Aren't you already?"

"Sometimes."

"Choose a side. Choose the winning side. The white side."

"You sound like Mama. She's drunk a few or she's stressed, you should hear her talk."

"I didn't say it was right. I said it's the better choice. Your brains and looks, you could do all right for yourself."

"You have brains and looks and you sell used cars. Shit, Ed. I shouldn't have said that. Didn't mean it. That was Mama talking. We both sound like her sometimes."

"Well, pains me to say it, but she's not altogether wrong."

(13)

I drove out there, Melinda giving me directions. It was well out in the woods, and there was an old house there and there were lights on inside of it, but the lights were from kerosene lamps, not electricity. I knew that kind of light. I had grown up with it. It was softer and warmer, and if you walked six feet away from the lamp in the dead of night, you couldn't find your ass with both hands.

The house itself looked as if it was one good windstorm from going flat. The porch sagged and the steps didn't quite connect to it. There were four cars in the yard. I didn't stop there but on down the road. I turned off the lights and engine, turned in the seat to look at Melinda's shadow shape. "That was it?"

"No. I'm just messing with you. It's a house I'm thinking of buying."

"Smart-ass. Okay. What's he look like?"

"Good-looking. Dapper. Wears a hat with a feather in it."

"What if another guy there has a feather?"

"I guess I better come with you."

"I don't know."

"You might talk to the wrong fellow."

44

"I might at that." I leaned over and got the little revolver out of the glove box and put it in my jacket pocket.

"That help you talk better?"

"I find it a comfort in case the talk stops talking."

We got out of the car and walked along a line of hickory trees and then we walked softly across the yard and up the porch steps. We went up them as quietly as possible, but they squeaked like a mouse. We stopped at the door.

No one seemed to have heard us.

The door was open and there was just the screen. All the windows along the porch were open, and they were screened. Bugs bounced against them. Mosquitoes buzzed in my ears.

"Stand right here," I said.

I went over and peeked in one of the windows. There were four men sitting around a table playing cards. There was a kerosene lamp on the table. There was money on the table too. No one was wearing a hat. No one saw me. They were too engrossed in their game.

I eased back to Melinda. "Come here. Be quiet about it."

I led her to the window and she looked in, then we walked back to the screen door.

"Well?"

"It's the man in the brown shirt. That's Cecil."

"Cecil, huh. Go back and wait in the car." I dug in my pocket and gave her the key. "Things don't go right, you drive away. He might not be in a talkative mood."

"Sometimes they carry guns."

"Like the one I got?"

"I just know they sometimes do."

"You been out here more than once, haven't you?"

"Maybe."

"We'll call this your last trip and I mean it. Go back to the car, please."

(14)

It wasn't a smart thing to do, but I was feeling pissed off about Mama and this guy making a deal with her for booze. I was pained by it on more levels than I could've explained if I had all night and a better vocabulary.

I eased the screen open and tiptoed down the hallway, through the door, and into the main room where the light was.

One of the men looked up and saw me. I saw him ease his hand under a coat lying on an empty chair next to him.

I pulled my pistol out and let it hang by my side, said, "I wouldn't. I'm not here to give you grief. I just want to talk to Cecil."

The lamplight lay on Cecil's face, and he was I guess what you would call handsome. His skin was black as night and he wore his years pretty good. I figured him to be fifty or so.

"I don't know you," Cecil said.

"I'm thinking you might like to."

"On account of?"

"I say so and I got a gun."

"We all got guns."

"Yeah, but I have mine drawn and I don't miss much." This wasn't true. I couldn't hit a house if I was in it.

"What you want with me?"

"It's not gunplay. This is just an insurance policy I have."

"Yeah. What you collect if you need it."

"Way it works is I don't collect nothing, but whoever gives me shit might collect bullets. Look here. I don't want trouble, and I got nothing to say to the rest of you. Just want to talk to Cecil, not shoot him."

"We got to believe that?" said the man who had made to reach beneath his coat.

"You don't got to, but you might want to."

"It's all right," Cecil said. "I want to see what this cracker is talking about. This about some booze?"

"It is."

"You must be wanting some bad, come out here like this this time of night, and with a pistol."

"Let's just say I get mighty thirsty."

Cecil stood up slowly and placed his cards facedown on the table. "You can deal me out. My hand couldn't be any worse if there was nothing but jokers in the deck."

"You sure?" said another of the men.

"Yeah. It's all right. Me and him just going to do some business."

"That's right," I said. I stuck my hand and the pistol in my coat pocket, but I didn't let go of it. I let it and my hand rest in there with my blackjack. I liked carrying that around on a regular basis. Call me nervous.

The other men started playing cards again. They were far more interested in that than a liquor transaction.

Cecil put on his hat. It had been resting on his knee. It had a white feather in it.

Me and Cecil went outside. He automatically walked toward his car, thinking I wanted to buy some booze. He put a key in the trunk lock and lifted it. There were wooden cases filled with fruit jars of a dark liquid. There was straw packed between the jars.

"You come out here late at night, and me busy, I got to boost the price."

"I said I wanted to talk, not buy."

"What the hell, fellow. You said you were thirsty."

"I did, didn't I? I lied a bit."

"On account of?"

"I got a drunk mother you sell booze to, and I want you to quit. And I sure want you to quit trading booze for something else."

Cecil let that float around inside his noggin for a while. "Oh, I know who you're talking about. That your mother? She's a fine-looking woman. Could dress up a bit. She's fine, though. Know what I mean?"

"Yeah. I know what you mean. And I don't want you messing with her. I don't want you selling her booze. Fact is, I don't want you over there at all. Your car breaks down a mile from her place, you better start walking the other way. Your dog sniffs around the door there, you better call him in and shoot him."

"That's some tough talk, there. You got a mirror at your house, boy? I'm twice your size. That gun, I'll take that away from you and jam it up your nose."

I pulled my hand out of my pocket quickly. I no longer had hold of the pistol. I had the blackjack. I caught him over the ear hard enough to knock him to his knees.

He put his hand to the side of his head, said, "Goddamn, man."

"Still want to take my gun? Want my blackjack?"

"I want you to leave my ass alone."

"You going to stay away from her?"

"I'm going to do what I want to do. You mad because she's white and I'm black. You don't like to think about that nigger dick in your sweet mama's pussy."

I hit him with the blackjack again. "Wrong answer."

"Goddamn, man. Sure. I'll leave her alone."

"You don't sound all that convincing." This time I hit him right on top of the head. He went forward and held himself up with his hands. "Am I starting to make myself clear?"

He threw up and began breathing heavily. "Yeah, man. I got you."

"I'm not sure you do."

I went to work on him a little. I don't know how many times I hit him, but it must have been three or four more. I tried to keep all the blows on his shoulders and ribs from then on.

He sat back on his ass then. His quivering hand reached under his coat. I stepped forward and hit him again and leaned down and took out a little Saturday-night special with my free hand and gave it a sling.

"I meant what I said. You don't go by there no more. I don't care if she wants it and sends a carrier pigeon with a fucking note telling you she does."

"All right, all right. It's done. I'm done. No booze for her. You looking crazy, man. You look like you so mad, you want to beat yourself. I don't know why you just can't leave a nigger alone."

"Don't call yourself that." I put the gun back in my pocket.

He looked up at me. "You a funny white boy."

I waved the blackjack. "Want me to have a few more laughs?"

Cecil held up his hand. "No. I've had enough."

About then, one of the men came out of the house and let the screen door slam. I could see the others bunched up behind the screen.

"What in hell is going on out here, Cecil? He hurting you?"

"Oh, it's all right. I done got a lifetime of that. It's all right."

The man outside the screen door moved toward the porch.

"Tell them to go back to their game or you won't be joining

them later." I dropped the blackjack back in my pocket and pulled out the pistol.

Cecil managed to stand up. I'll give him this. Had that been most people, they couldn't have gotten up after that. He was bleeding under his ear and under his nose. I didn't even remember catching him there.

"You got something wrong inside of you, boy," he said.

"You go on with your game, now. Just do like I asked, and me and you won't be visiting anymore."

"That's news I like hearing," he said and started back toward the house.

I walked out to the road, and when I got there the lights from my car were coming my way. Melinda picked me up and we drove out of there.

(15)

We drove to Mama's house trailer and parked out front. Melinda kept sitting behind the wheel.

"I got a feeling that wasn't just a talk."

"It had some argumentative moments."

"Daddy was like that. He would start to talk, and next thing you knew you were on the ground with loose teeth. He knocked me over a couch once. Remember that?"

"I do."

"I was damn little. You were older, and you tried to fight him, and he knocked you down."

"I remember that part really well."

"He called us his little snowflake fuckers."

"I remember that too."

"You think about this, Ed. Someone finds out you got a drop of colored in you, all of a sudden you're colored, and that's it. You want to play that game all your life, lying to yourself and everyone around you? Trying to be white?"

"We are white. Look at us. Shit, Melinda. I got a good job and a Cadillac out of lighter skin."

"Who you are chases you, is what I think," Melinda said. "I don't believe there is anywhere you can go where you'll stay white. We decide to be black, that doesn't work out well either, even if we are driving a Cadillac."

"I'll play the game as long as I can get away with it," I said. "How do you think it works we play the other side? We're caught in the middle and squeezed from the sides."

"I guess so."

"You got to play it too, baby. The game is already set, and the winning side has lighter skin."

"Our own brother doesn't have anything much to do with us, Ed. Maybe in your case, nothing to do with you at all, and you like it that way. We don't even know him. Not really. Mama loves him, but she doesn't want us tainted with his blackness."

"She's just being realistic. I don't like it that way, but it's for the best for all of us, so that's how we play it. Up north, they don't have the signs on water fountains and above toilet doors that say Colored, but they got places they can't go because they're dark-skinned. It may be better in Detroit, but it's not like it ought to be, and me and you, we don't have to worry about that. We can go anywhere and do anything we want without a *Green Book* to guide the way. It may not be right, baby sister, but that's how it is. Life doesn't have balance, just extremes."

"I'll see you, Ed. But not too soon, okay?"

Melinda got out. I watched her go up the steps and into the house trailer. I put the pistol back in the glove box, slid over behind the wheel, and pulled away from there.

(16)

When I got back to my place, there was a note stuck in the door handle. I pulled it out and looked at it under the porch light.

COME BY AND SEE ME TOMORROW. AT THE DRIVE-IN. FIVE P.M. WEAR TIGHT PANTS. N.

I went inside and got myself a beer out of the refrigerator and then I thought about Mama and tonight and how I had enjoyed hitting Cecil with that blackjack and how right he was about how mad I was, and about how I was so mad it was like I wanted to hit myself. He was just being a smart-ass, but he was righter than he realized.

It ran through my mind about Mama in her bedroom smoking cigarettes and trembling from lack of booze, looking up at me, her disappointment of a son who ought to be doing better because his black-skinned brother was doing well, and he didn't even have the advantage of looking white. I thought about Melinda, how smart she was for her age, what she could learn if she could get out of that trailer, get educated, find a decent job.

I put the beer back and got an ice tray and emptied it into a plastic bowl and used some of the ice to half fill a glass. I poured iced tea from a pitcher into the glass. I had melted about a half a cup of sugar in the pitcher when I'd made the batch and it was hot. It was some damn sweet stuff.

I filled the tray with water and put it back in the freezer part of the refrigerator, put the pitcher back where I got it, then went and sat down on the couch. I thought about getting up and turning on the TV set but didn't do it. All of a sudden, I felt tired and worn out and unreal.

I sipped the tea slowly. It was good and cold and it took some of the heat out of me. Heat from the weather and from what I had done. When the tea was all gone, I read Nancy's note again, then went to the bedroom. I took off my sports coat and felt the black-jack sliding around in the coat pocket. I took it out and saw that it had blood on it. I washed it in the bathroom sink, watched as bits of red went down the drain. I felt a little sick seeing that.

I dampened a rag and turned my coat pocket inside out, and as I suspected, there were drops of blood in it. I used the damp rag with cold water to clean it. I got most of it out. There was a little darkened stain left, but it didn't go through onto the outside of the coat. I put the rag away and hung the coat up in the closet.

I stripped off naked and got in bed. I pulled the sheet and blanket up to my chest. I left the bedside lamp on so I could read. I picked up a book I had been reading off the nightstand, then put it down. I didn't want to read.

I thought about seeing Nancy tomorrow and I could almost smell her.

(17)

Next morning, I felt sluggish. All night long I had awakened from dreams about that man I had hit with the blackjack. I couldn't decide if I was waking up because I was sick over what I had done or if I was excited about it. After I showered, I looked in my closet and picked my best outfit. I didn't have any tight pants. What I had was a dark pair that had a nice crease. I wore a light blue shirt with a blue and red sports coat and no tie and a blackjack in the pocket. My shoes were black and well shined. I had learned how to shine shoes from my father. He had shined shoes for a living, at least some of the time, in a barbershop in Gladewater, Texas. He had his own stand in there. When I thought about that, I felt a lot like an impostor. I'd told Dave my father had died when I was young and that he had been an engineer.

I stood in front of the mirror.

I looked like a used-car salesman. I looked like one every day, but that day the realization landed on me like pigeon shit.

I wanted to look like what I wanted to be: A man who owned a Cadillac and might own a drive-in theater and a pet cemetery where maybe you didn't throw the pets in the woods. Someone with a good-looking blonde on his arm that made other men turn their heads and look.

I decided then and there, after work, I would go over to James's Men's Wear and buy myself some nice clothes. I had enough money for that. I had enough money for a lot of things, but I wouldn't have minded a lot more of it. Mama always said money made you glow, and right then, I didn't glow.

When I got to work that morning, Dave was standing in the lot smoking a cigar. There was a tall man with him wearing a hat and a brown suit.

I got out of the car, and as I was heading to the office, I passed them. I heard Dave giving part of his spiel.

"Man dresses nice like you do, well, you ought to have a car matches the suit. Something makes you stand out when you're driving along. Something makes you look like what you are. Successful."

I went on up to the office and hung my coat over the back of a chair and started making coffee. While I was doing that, I looked out the window and watched as Dave walked the man around the lot.

They stopped at a bright green Buick that I knew was actually a pretty good car. It probably wouldn't fall apart in a week, but the odometer had been turned back by me, and the tires had been shoeblacked to make them look fresher. They had tread, but they weren't good tires.

After a bit Dave and the man came into the office. I poured Dave and the man a cup of coffee apiece and offered some sugar to them. We didn't have cream, and I didn't want to be a waiter.

Dave sat behind his desk and the man sat in front of it.

"So, thing is too," Dave said, "car has room for your wife and kids, and you still got enough space in there to add a kid."

"Oh," said the man, "I think we're calling in the dogs on the kids. I think two is plenty."

"I hear that," Dave said. "Kids are costly, and you want to be able to give them the attention they deserve."

"We have family days," said the man. "We go out to the lake and picnic, to movies, now and then to a nice restaurant, though no one complains about Dairy Queen."

"I like a good hamburger, as you can tell," Dave said and patted his stomach.

They went on a little more, then got down to brass tacks about the contract, and the man sounded like he knew a thing or two, so Dave didn't try to pull a thing or two.

What I was thinking about was having a wife and a kid and a picnic. Basic American dream, except mine included someone else's wife and the businesses that went with it.

I sold one car that day and kind of flubbed another sale because my mind wasn't on it. At the end of the day, as I was putting on my coat, Dave said, "Ed, you do fine, but I tell you, I thought you had that other sale in the bag."

He had been out in the lot wiping dust off the cars, which for Dave was real work, fat as he was. He had heard me talking to this woman who wanted a car to drive to an out-of-town job four days a week. I talked her up good. She was a little fat lady in a loose dress with flower decorations on it. It was just one step up from a muumuu. I could tell she liked me, liked what she saw, and I tried to work that.

"Just couldn't close it out," I said.

"You seemed like you wanted to be somewhere else. You know what I say about that?"

"Yeah. When you're selling a car, that's all you do until they sign on the dotted line. It's not like it's a magnificent saying, Dave."

"No, but it's true."

He was right. I'd had that sale in my pocket, and through in-attention, not answering some simple questions right, not smiling enough, and, in the end, not flirting enough, I had lost it. I was thinking about that new suit and Nancy, that's what I was thinking about. It would have been nice to have had the sale to afford the suit, but there you have it. I was inattentive.

"I'll get it next time," I said.

"Hey, just saying, not complaining. We all have a day when we miss a step. Had a couple come in once, saw the car they wanted right away, a sure sale, and I talked them out of it. Problem was I couldn't talk them into another one, and there was no going back to the other. I had made it sound inferior to what they were looking for because I could sell them another I could make more money off of. Sometimes you think you're so good at something, you can outsmart yourself."

"Guess so," I said.

I put on my coat and drove over to the suit shop. I looked around for a while and then, with the assistance of the saleslady, I found what I wanted, tried it on, looked in the mirror.

I liked it. I looked like a man that owned a business and didn't need anyone's help.

I bought the suit, some shirts to go with it, a couple of ties, and I bought some everyday clothes as well.

I drove home and put on the suit again and stood in front of the mirror for a while, then I put the suit away and picked out a pair of nice dark slacks I had bought and a blue pullover shirt. I laid them out on the bed, went and took a long shower.

I spent extra time combing my hair, which I had let grow out a little bit so there was enough to come back on the sides and the top. For a while after I got out of the military, I wore it cut short, but I had seen the way John Kennedy wore his hair, and I thought I could look a little like him with the right clothes and the right style of hair.

I brushed my teeth and gargled some mouthwash, then drove out to the High-Tone Drive-In.

(18)

You could see the light from the drive-in long before you got to the actual HIGH-TONE sign that made the light. As you drove closer, you saw the sign sticking up above a line of trees that went around a curve in the road. It was pretty tall, and I want to say again that at night it looked like a shiny finger pointing to the heavens, and the light made a gold path through the night sky and lay across the inside of the drive-in entrance and in front of the concession stand like a pool of molten honey.

That light was brighter than the other drive-in lights, the ones from the concession and the ones on the marquee that shone on the black letters that announced a dusk-to-dawn extravaganza with a list of movie titles.

I parked my car on the road and studied that light. I watched it for a time, watched a line of cars going in. I sat there and thought about how much money that was per car. A ticket was cheap, but you add a lot of cars, toss in concession sales, and it could be pretty sweet.

I imagined myself standing right in front of that place, looking up at the sign, and I thought about how I could just walk back to Nancy's house every night and how it would be my house too.

It was just imagining, but I had been imagining a lot, and the imagining was getting louder, like there was a bass drum thumping behind it.

I drove up and went through the line like everyone else. There was a man in the booth, a nice-looking guy with a small purple birthmark on his cheek. He looked tough as a boar hog.

When he said, "One?," as if that wasn't obvious, I said, "Is Mrs. Craig here? I thought I might see her on a bit of business. I sold her a car."

"You seeing the pictures?"

"No. I just need to see her. She asked for me to come out."

"Did she?"

"Yes. I'm Ed Edwards. She'll know."

"Will she?"

I was starting to get a bit irritated. A line of cars was forming behind me. The car in back of me, full of loud-talking teenagers, honked.

"All right, but I better not find you on the lot."

"I wanted to sneak into the drive-in, I'd have a better plan than that, pal. I can give up a dollar and not cry about it if that's your worry."

"Go on in," he said, "and pull over in front of the concession."

There were only a few places to park at the concession. I picked one and got out. I looked up at the big tall screen and the cars that were rambling about, finding places to park beside the speaker posts. That drive-in held a lot of cars.

Inside the concession, I saw Nancy right away. She was behind the counter with a young pimple-faced woman who was handling the popcorn and such. Nancy looked up at me and smiled a little. She didn't give the full smile much, but when she did, those nice teeth made me wish they were nibbling somewhere on me.

There were several teenagers at the counter, and as I came

through the door and stepped aside, more showed up. They were buying hot dogs and popcorn, candy and sodas like a pack of hungry wolves with wallets. Thing like that, depending on the concession's cut, could add up.

She said something to the girl and came out from behind the counter. She had on a sharp-looking blue top and an ice-blue short skirt and low-heeled, open-toed blue shoes. She said, "Did you bring the car papers?"

"Yes," I said, playing along with whatever was going on.

"We can talk about it in the office."

I followed her through an open door by the concession to a small room with a cleared desk, two chairs, and some odds and ends on a couple of shelves. One shelf held a cardboard box of files and a small fan. The fan had a long cord and it was plugged in, but it wasn't on. I noticed that under her left eye, she was wearing quite a bit of makeup. It had caked a little.

"This is private business, Mr. Edwards. Could you close the door?"

She said that a little loud so it would be overheard. I closed the door.

"Lock it," she said.

I locked it.

Nancy hiked her skirt over her hips. She wasn't wearing any underwear. She sat back on the desk and spread her legs.

She knew where I was looking. She smiled at me. This time I got the whole thing, and let me tell you, when she turned it on full-teeth, it was a powerful thing, but not as powerful as what was between her legs.

"I thought it would save time," she said.

I went to her, unbuckling my belt. She grabbed my crotch and unzipped me, and then she pulled at me, and I went forward and inside her. She grabbed my shoulders, kissed me, wrapped her legs around me.

I was like a starving man finally having dinner. I was like a thirsty man with a bucket of fresh-cranked well water. I was like a drowning man reaching for a hunk of debris to float on.

We were breathing heavy, holding in the screams we wanted to make, and it went on and on, and finally she made a kind of grunt and a sigh, and I followed with something similar.

After kissing softly, we separated. I pulled up my pants and took a deep breath. I needed it. She slipped off the desk and pulled her skirt down. It smelled musky in there.

She went behind the desk, opened it, pulled out a box of matches, and struck a few. "Turn on the fan."

I turned on the fan. It started to rotate. It had grown hot and stuffy in the room.

"Unlock the door."

I unlocked the door.

We waited there a moment, her standing behind the desk, me on the other side. We were looking at each other.

Her eyelids were heavy; her voice was husky. "I couldn't wait anymore."

"I'm glad you couldn't," I said.

"I've been thinking, thinking a lot."

"Oh." I hate to admit it, but I already had some inkling of where this was going, though I was hoping that wasn't where it was going at all.

(19)

She sat down behind the desk and I pulled the other chair over and sat in front of it and looked at her.

"He's home."

"Frank."

"Yeah. Him. Who else would I mean?"

"How long has he been back?"

"A while. I didn't think you needed to know until I was sure I wanted to see you. I guess I was always sure, but I tried not to jump at the idea. I knew it could get messy. But now that he's home, I'm certain of what I figured I was certain of. I hate him." She touched a finger to her heavily made-up eye. "He did this."

"He hit you?"

"He always hits me. Usually it's to the body so it doesn't show, and he did that too, and then this eye shot. He's getting careless because he's getting drunker every time he's back in."

"Why did he hit you?"

"Doesn't need a reason, but this time it was the Cadillac."

"Because I took it back?"

"Yeah, that. For God's sake, quit being dense."

Her demeanor had changed. I felt like an employee about to get the boot.

"He doesn't need a missing Cadillac to hit me, though. All he needs is for him to be him."

"I see."

"I don't know if you do."

I did, but I was playing dumb. Right then, I knew I needed to leave and not come back, but I sat there as if I were made of lead.

"You like me, right?" she asked.

"I think I just proved that."

"That's one thing, but then there's the other."

"The like part?"

"I was thinking the love part."

"Is that where we are?"

"I'm thinking we could get there."

"Except you're married."

"That's the problem."

"Okay, get unmarried, you don't want to stay with him. Get unmarried, and you and me can see how things play out."

She shook her head. "Listen to me, Ed. I can tell a lot about a man pretty quick."

I didn't doubt that.

"I think you're a man that likes fucking me and I think you're a man wants to move up in life."

"Fair enough."

"What I'm thinking, we could both do all right by each other. I wasn't married to Frank, you and me could run this drive-in together, the cemetery, branch out into other businesses. I mean, hell, you could own your own car lot."

"I don't know I want to keep selling cars."

"Goddamn it, Ed. Are you listening?"

"I think so. I mean, I hear you."

"No. You don't. You won't sell cars, you'll have someone sell them for you, and the drive-in, it's a good nest egg, even the pet cemetery is. People pay some pretty silly money for us to mound up some dirt and throw their mutts in the woods. What we could have, Frank wasn't taking it all to drink and whore on the road, we could use to open a car lot, and you could hire people to sell cars for you. That would be three businesses. This drive-in business. I don't see an end to it. People got to drive cars, and there's a few people want to bury their pets for silly money. I think we could be rich, all of it was handled right, and it isn't."

"We still got that whole you're-married problem."

"I'm coming to that. You see, something happens to Frank, I got a nice insurance policy, and I got a will made up, and I can sign his name really well, and I know a notary I can show it to, say, 'Oh, Frank forgot to file this, wrote it up himself, signed it, but didn't notarize it, can you do that?' I think he will, I smile right."

"I think he will too," I said. "Let me make a guess. That insurance policy and, obviously, the will, he's got to be dead for that. He sick?"

"Far from it."

"I figured that."

"Shit, Ed. You know what I'm saying."

"I know what you're saying, all right, and I'm not getting into that."

"You were in the war, weren't you?"

"How'd you know?"

"Because it's likely. You kill anybody?"

"From afar, and because they were trying to kill me." That wasn't entirely true. It hadn't all been from afar, but I didn't want to get into that.

"Frank keeps on, one day he'll kill me. Last time he was in, he hit me hard enough in the kidney I was pissing blood for a week. Eventually, he'll do me in."

"Where is he now?"

"Honky-tonk. He comes in, hits me, fucks me, has a sandwich and a beer, then goes out to the tonks. He comes in next morning smelling of perfume and pussy. Sometimes he takes me right then. I usually get a few more punches. He always thinks I'm cheating on him."

"You are."

"But with good reason. He was all right when I married him. Big, handsome guy and I thought he was going places, bought this drive-in, but after a bit, it kind of runs itself, and he's taking the profit and leaving me home, going out on the road to fuck and drink and sell some encyclopedias. I told him, 'Quit the door-to-door, let's run these businesses right,' but he's not interested. He doesn't sell *World Book* for the money. He takes the profit from this stuff, mostly. Salesman job gives him an excuse to hang with his buddies, chase whores. I know he's sold some sets, but I've never seen a dime from it. He found out about the Cadillac being gone, he went over to Luther's Motors and bought him a Ford, paid down on it with bill money. Now he'll quit making the payments on that and put us in hotter water."

"Luther sells shittier cars than we do."

"I got no future with him, Ed."

"Let's get back to that whole insurance-and-will part, quit beating around the bush and get that out of the way, because I'm not liking that. It smells like prison and my ass frying in the electric chair. That's not much of a future for either one of us."

"If you get caught."

"Murderers always get caught."

"Except the ones get away with it. Think about it, Ed. We

only know about the ones that get caught, ones that make a stupid mistake."

"Got a feeling we might end up in that pile."

"Listen. I want you. You want me. We can make that work if we get rid of Frank, and unlike him, you can run a business the way it's supposed to be run. We'd have an empire in this town, a string of drive-ins and car lots, good clothes, good cars, lots of spending money."

"It's a string of drive-ins now, multiple car lots. You got it all worked out, don't you?"

"Well, I don't quite have how Frank dies worked out, but I've got some ideas that just need fine-tuning."

"Well, I've enjoyed seeing you with your panties off, and I'm feeling pretty refreshed, but this other business, I don't want anything to do with that."

About then there was a knock on the door.

"Come in," Nancy said.

It was the guy from the ticket stand. Looking at him standing in the doorway, I could see he was pretty good-sized.

He studied us for a moment.

"What is it, Walter?"

"I think we got a lull in the tickets, show's going on and all. I put the chain up, thought I'd grab a hot dog and such."

"Sure."

"All right." But he didn't move away from the doorway. "Anything I can do for you before I take my break?"

"I don't think so. Pardon my manners. Walter, this is Ed Edwards. Ed, this is Walter Wood, a cousin of mine. He works for me."

"We met," I said.

"Of course. All right, Walter. Take your break."

He moved away from the doorway, into the concession area. He left the door open.

"Think on it some," she said.

"I already have, and I already don't like it."

I got up and didn't look at her. I didn't say anything. I left out of there and walked to the car feeling like I had dodged one hell of a large and powerful bullet. I was afraid if I turned and looked at her, saw her face, I might not make the effort to dodge.

(20)

A few days went by, and then late at night, I was awakened by the phone ringing. I rolled out of bed, sleepy and pissed, and answered it.

"Ed. It's Nancy."

"I thought me and you were done."

"I didn't say that."

"Yeah, but I thought what you asked me did it in."

"Frank beat me up. I'm at a phone booth. He beat me up pretty bad, and when he was asleep, I slipped off. I took my car. I didn't know where I was going, just driving, but then it broke down. I'm at a closed filling station. I can't get the car started, and I'm out here alone. It's not a good spot."

"Relax. Call a wrecker service."

"I'm calling you."

"And I'm telling you to call a wrecker service."

"I don't have money for it. Frank has all the money. I mean, I got a few dollars."

"Call a taxi."

"Goddamn it, Ed, really."

"Shit. Where exactly are you?"

I got dressed and drove out to where she was. It was a filling station off the main highway. It was dark except for some lights around the doorway, a dim one behind the plate-glass window, and some lights on the gas pumps. She was standing by the phone booth at the corner of the station. Her car was parked nearby.

I got out and she walked over to me. "It just quit."

I took her key and tried to start it. It wouldn't start. I looked under the hood. The radiator was steaming.

I put the hood down.

"You get in and guide the wheel," I said. "I'm going to push it over to the water hose."

The water hose was between the two pumps, and she got in behind the wheel and put it in neutral, and I pushed it. I damn near ruptured myself until I got it rolling and then it was easy.

When she parked, I opened the hood again, and, using a rag I had from the Cadillac, I screwed the lid off the radiator and jumped back when it spit a gusher of hot water and steam filled the air.

The night was clear, but the steam was thick, and Nancy came from the side of the car, walking through the steam that had fanned out in all directions.

It was kind of eerie, seeing her come through that steam, and then she was beside me and the steam was turning clear.

I sprayed the radiator with the hose to cool it down and then I ran water into it, put the lid on it. After a bit I saw the water leaking out of the radiator in a small stream.

"We need to have it set a minute," I said.

"I didn't know who else to call."

"It's okay. You got a hole in the radiator. Let it cool, I got some stuff to pour in it. I've done it with a lot of used cars, always carry some with me. We can put more water in after that. It'll get you to the house, and you can drive it around a while, but you need a new radiator."

She was near one of the gas pumps now, and I could see her face better, and it was a banged-up face, both eyes blacked. She had a small trickle of dried blood under her nose.

"Damn. He did a number on you."

"I thought he was going to kill me."

"Why'd he do it?"

"He wanted sex and I didn't want to give it to him. He got sex, and I got this."

Thinking about her husband raping her made my skin crawl.

"I'm afraid he's going to kill me, but I don't know what to do. I don't have money. I don't have anything."

We went over and sat in my Cadillac.

We didn't say anything for a long time. She scooted over and leaned on me and I put my arm around her.

She smelled like sweat and blood, a dash of sweet perfume.

"Jesus, Ed. I would be so grateful."

Nancy said that out of the blue, but I knew what she was talking about.

"I can't keep going through this. This time I hurt all over, and he wasn't trying to avoid my face. I think he's working himself up. He drinks so much, he's crazy half the time. Next time, he just might kill me."

I was surprised that I answered right away.

"Not if we kill him first."

(21)

I got her car going, had her drive it to my place, told her to park down the block from the address I gave her.

She parked on the street and I pulled up beside her. She got in the Caddy, carrying her purse, and I drove us down the block, parked, and we hustled inside my apartment.

When I turned on the light, Nancy looked around. "It's neater than I expected."

"Yeah?"

"Most bachelors are pretty messy."

"I don't have a lot to make a mess with. You want a drink?"

"I could use it."

"First, let's go in the bathroom and wash up your face."

I used a hand towel with a bit of warm water on it to clean away the blood under her nose and at the corner of her mouth. I gave her a towel, and she took a hot shower.

Wearing the towel, she joined me in the kitchen. I gave her a couple aspirin with a glass of water and then I broke the ice out of the refrigerator freezer, poured most of it into a dish towel, bunched the towel around the cubes, and gave it to her to press against her eyes.

I said, "You'll have to take turns. Five minutes on one, five minutes on the other, rotate until the ice melts."

She started with the left eye.

I dropped a couple of spare cubes in some small glasses and poured us some whiskey. I didn't water it down. The cubes would do that well enough.

We sat at the kitchen table, her holding the ice-filled towel to her eye with one hand, the whiskey with the other.

I sipped mine, said, "What's he going to do, he wakes up and finds you gone?"

"Probably more of what he just did. Couple times before, I ran off for a day or so, and it wasn't even this bad. I'm starting to get sore all over. He hit me a good one in the kidney. I figure I'll be pissing blood again. He caught me one in the chest, on my left tit, and I felt like my heart skipped a beat. I actually quit breathing for a moment. A lung seized up."

"So now you're a doctor."

"No, I'm experienced with pain. I just won't go back for a while."

"You can stay here tonight."

"I appreciate that. What you said——"

"I might have been hasty when I said it."

"Don't crawfish on me."

"Killing someone, that's a big thing, and it's a heavy burden. In Korea I killed some people who were trying to kill me. I did what I had to do, but this, I don't have to do it."

"So you're saying now you won't do it?"

"What I'm saying, Nancy, is we can't go about this half-assed. We got to have a plan that makes it look like an accident."

"Then you have thought about it."

"Yeah. I have thought about it, but I don't have it worked out, not the nitty-gritty of it. Just the big picture, but we got to have the big and the small, we're going to do this."

"It would change my life."

"It would change both of our lives, but I'm not sure for the better."

"Then why consider it?"

I was wondering that myself, but I knew the answer. I wanted the woman and I wanted the businesses, and mostly I wanted a shot to do well, better than my father did, better than my brother, and better than my mother would expect. I wanted a white man's shot.

I had been thinking about what Nancy said about an empire. We could have kids. We could have a good life. And what was Frank anyway but a wifebeater? A drunk and an asshole blowing the money from the businesses, businesses me and Nancy could run a lot better.

Not everyone deserved to live. Some people pave a short path to hell, and I had decided Frank was one of them.

(22)

We tried to make love, but she was too sore to enjoy it, so we had to give up. She lay in the crook of my arm and we watched the ceiling fan overhead beat around in a circle.

"What I'm thinking," I said, "is Frank has a little accident."

"What kind of accident?"

"I've been running that around in my mind, and I thought first it might be something electrical or an accidental fire in the home, but then again, that would burn up your home."

"Yeah, I don't like that idea."

"Me either. Electricity, that's tricky. I think what we got to do is have him have a car wreck, have that kill him."

"You going to ask him to drive his car off a cliff?"

"I think I might have to persuade him a little. I thought about it a lot, but the thing is, you'd have to put up with him a little bit, and we'd really have to play it cool for a while."

"I'm listening."

"Does Frank fish? I saw a little motorboat in the garage, so I thought he might."

"Now and again."

"Does he have a rod and reel?"

"In the barn where we park the cars. Behind the boat."

"Okay, so what I'm thinking is — you know Mason Creek?"

"No."

"It's a big creek well down in the woods but not so well down in the woods someone won't come along in time and see him. There's a wooden bridge over it, and the rails look like the only thing holding them together is termites. I'm thinking, he goes to fish, maybe he's drunk as a high-school reunion, and he loses control of the car, goes through the rails and into the water. Creek is deep there under the bridge. I fished there a couple times. Only thing wrong with it is, I kept catching fish. I hate cleaning them."

"How do we get him out there? How do we get him to go through the rails, and who says that will kill him? Hell, he can swim like a fish."

"Dead fish don't swim. You see, we might have to help him a little before he goes out there. How long is he going to be home?"

"A while, but he'll mostly be at the tonks come night. Then the rest of his agenda is come home, beat and fuck me, and go to sleep. At some point, he hits the road again."

"Save up his beer cans, liquor bottles, what have you, pack them away somewhere. We need a bunch."

"Why would I do that?"

"Because I plan to put a lot of them in his car so when he goes through the railing, it looks like he's drunk enough to do that. In fact, you got to get him drunk."

"Like I said, he comes home drunk. He doesn't need my help. I like it when he's real drunk 'cause he can't hit too hard, and after he hits me awhile, he falls to sleep and I don't get fucked. Or raped is more like it."

She started crying a little.

"It's all right, baby. It's all falling into place. We're going to fix that bastard up, collect that insurance money, then you and me, we're going to shoot for the stars."

(23)

It was a pretty simple plan, really, as I figure it's best not to complicate things. I was actually starting to feel excited about it. A little scared, yeah, but nothing like Korea. That was fear, all right. This, well, it was really about being clever. It was the same as convincing someone to buy a used car they neither wanted nor needed, make them think it was just the thing for them. This was about making things look one way when they were another. Emotional sleight-of-hand.

As we lay in bed, Nancy hardly able to move from the beating she took, we gradually put it together. I had some of it, but she had some of it too.

"How often does he drink?"

"How often is it night?"

"Does he always get stone drunk?"

"Always."

"Here's what I'm thinking. He gets stone drunk, comes home, and we let him do that a couple of days, and you got to do your best to avoid him."

"I always do my best. Maybe I could sleep in the office at the drive-in."

"Can't let him suspect anything. We let him come home a couple of nights, get in a pattern, and the next night, when he goes out, I park somewhere down the road and come over. We put his fishing gear handy in the house where he can't see it. Then we wait for him to come home. I'll wait in the closet with a blackjack."

"You'll need more than a blackjack. He's big, Ed. Really big, and stout. We were out at a bar one night, and someone looked at me in a way he didn't like, and he fought that man and his two buddies, went through them like shit through a goose. He's tough, all right."

"I'll bring a crowbar or something. I'll wait in the bedroom closet, and when the time is right, I'll come out of it and hit him in the back of the head. We'll have the lightbulb out overhead, so he tries to switch it on, he can't, and then when I come out of the closet, I'll go for the home run. He's down and not dead, we got to have a plastic bag handy to put over his head, try and take the air out of him."

"Yeah, and who's going to hold him down while we put a plastic bag over his head?"

"A good lick from a crowbar ought to help us with that. Thing is, we don't want him too banged up. It's got to look like it was the car accident."

"All right, but swing hard."

"We get him smothered, and then we put him in his car along with the fishing gear, you see. You got to drive the car out to the creek, and I'll follow. Your story is that he left the next morning, early, to go fishing. What we do is we put him behind the wheel, set his car up so it runs into the bridge, breaks the barriers, goes over into the deep part of the creek."

"What then?"

"We go home and wait till someone discovers him. It might

take a while, but we wait. Stay away from each other during that time."

"I don't like that."

"Me either, baby, but we got to say later, when we're together, that we met when you bought a used car, and later, when your husband died, I saw you out at the drive-in, and there was a kind of spark, and we connected."

"Damn convenient."

"We got to wait at least a month. It'll seem less convenient then."

"A month?"

"Yeah, because you're not going to file for the insurance right away. You're going to be too distraught. That way it doesn't look like you're trying to clean up, shows you're in no hurry. A month or so later, you apply for the insurance for the accident, and then we've got our nest egg. We can see each other. Someone might not like it, but by then he'll be gone. Have him cremated. Don't want some wise-ass insurance investigator having him dug up, checking out this and that, comparing what did him in to how the accident happened and so on. Have him cremated right away."

"Do they do that here."

"One place and one place only. The colored funeral home on Elgin."

"Oh, hell, Ed. I don't know. I mean, it's one thing to kill him, but having him cremated in a colored funeral home, that looks like I don't care enough to have him cremated in a white funeral home."

"There isn't one."

"I know, but . . ."

I felt a snake of pain crawl around inside of me, and for a moment I wanted to tell her that she was a lot closer to colored than she thought, and then I thought about how she was when she was in bed when she wasn't broken and how much money that drive-in and cemetery could make, and about that empire, and I thought too about what my mother said about how I should be doing better, not having any color barriers on me, and I thought about my sister and some money for college, how she was smart and how she would have a real shot, and I caught my breath gently and just kept holding her.

When you're sniffing at true success, you can manage somehow not to smell the shit on the other side of the fence. I had learned that from Dave.

I said, "Listen here. We'll have him cremated in Tyler. I bet they have a crematorium there. I'll find out."

"Okay."

"Not one, then it's the funeral home on Elgin."

"You know, I don't mind it's a colored place, but I'm thinking others will look at it, decide I just wanted to get rid him, down to the point of using that funeral home that a white person might not use."

"Well, I die, you can have me cremated there. I don't mind."

"Don't even say that."

"Here's the thing. We got to really play it cool until you get the insurance money. You want to call me before we do this, call me when there's no chance he'll hear you. He's home, I don't care if he's sleeping, you go over to the drive-in and call from the office. No one's there during the day, right?"

"Walter sometimes. He does odd jobs. But mostly, yeah, I can do that."

"Let me know when he's gotten comfortable being home, and then we'll do it."

(24)

Nancy left shortly thereafter, said she would go to the drive-in, wait until he had slept it off. He'd sleep late, and he'd be apologies and sweetness, wanting her to fix him some breakfast, and she planned on doing it. And then he'd want to take her to bed, sore as she was, she said, and just the thought of it made me want to get my blackjack and pistol and walk in on him and shoot him until I had to reload. Beat him with the blackjack even if he was dead. But I had to grit my teeth, bide my time, and try and think about something else.

After she left, I had some coffee, too much of it, and then phoned work, told Dave I needed a day off to get some things done. He wasn't too crazy about that, working the place alone. He'd rather just take his cut as owner than walk around all day. He'd sell a car now and then to keep his hand in, and he was good at it, but walking the lot all day, he was too fat and his feet were bad.

"Look, I maybe can come in this afternoon, two or three hours before closing."

The lot was sometimes open until seven p.m., us trying to catch late sales, people who could only come by after work.

"I guess it's all right."

"I haven't taken a day off in ages. Left a little early a couple of times, but I'm selling cars for you just fine. Because of me, you got some serious take-home."

There was a silent moment of consideration and then Dave said, "All right, then, but come as early as you can. I've been a little off my feed lately."

"Sure. Hey, Dave, I didn't try and fake you out with a sick claim. I just need to get some stuff done."

"Good enough," he said.

I hadn't wanted to call in sick because I thought someone might see me around town, say something to Dave, and then it would be worse. It was better he thought I was just taking care of personal business, which, in fact, I was.

I drove over to the hardware store, bought myself a nice, heavy crowbar, but one of the smaller ones, so I could carry it easy enough, swing it without too much work. Still, you wouldn't have wanted to catch the business end of it if someone was swinging it at you.

I had my laundry with me, and I took it to the cleaners and checked it in, said I could use a couple plastic laundry bags.

They were a little big to use, if your plan was to smother someone, but I thought I could put one inside the other, fold them down at the open edge and make them easier to handle, easier to fit over an incapacitated man's head. It would hold in some of the blood from a head wound too. And that made me think of another thing.

I drove back to the hardware store, and me and the guy there joked how I was getting old, forgetting things, because I told him I needed a large painter's tarp, and I even bought paint and brushes to go with it. That meant I'd have to paint my bathroom or something, have something to show if I was asked, because I might be. Someone might say they saw me and her together and why did I buy a crowbar, and a tarp might even come up if you had some diligent police officer checking around for things like that; it could happen. I could point to the paint in my storage closet and the freshly painted bathroom and say, "Because of that. I got a tarp so I could drape it over the floor and the tub, not get paint everywhere, and I got the crowbar to pry off the door frame so I could replace it and paint it. But I decided that I could clean it and not have to replace it. Didn't need to replace it. Cleaning and painting were fine enough."

I was thinking it was just the kind of stupid thing a guy didn't know better might do. Some home-repair guy who decided he couldn't carpenter enough to replace the door trim so in the end, he just went with it. And I could also point to a few places where it was cracked around near the door hinge to show why I'd thought it needed replacing, even if in the end I didn't.

"Where's the tarp, Edwards?" the cops might ask, and I could say: "Tarp? Oh, yeah, the tarp. Well, hell, the dump." And it would be there too. I could soak it down in the tub first, clean it up a little, then take it to the dump, that way if they found it, I would have cleaned the blood off of it.

You see, I was thinking things through pretty good. I could use that tarp to put over the bed so as not to get blood on the sheets and mattress, because something like that, it would be a bitch to replace and not have some cop wonder why there was a new mattress on the bed.

Frank comes in and tries the light switch, it doesn't work, and Nancy says, "Just come to bed, Frank, we'll get a fresh bulb in the morning." He would know his way enough in the dark to start there, and then I'd come out of the closet, not throwing shadows with the light out, and I'd hit him. Blood sprayed, the floor and walls could be cleaned, but that mattress, that was a whole different sort of pickle.

Yeah. I was thinking good now. I let those thoughts ramble about in my skull for a moment.

The more I thought about killing him, more certain I was I could do it. I had once killed a Korean soldier with the butt of a rifle, and that had been close and goddamn personal. I never mentioned that. I always talked about the ones I had killed from afar. I didn't talk about it because I could still see his face, the way his eyes froze in his head and he twitched and then stopped twitching.

Sometimes, I went to bed, closed my eyes, I saw him again. I killed him over and over.

I kept telling myself that it had been him or me, and I believed it. This time, though, would be different.

I'd be killing for girl and profit, a somewhat more violent and bloodier version of the American dream.

(25)

I stopped by the library, had the librarian show me where they kept the yearly promotion books for the colleges and junior colleges in Texas. The librarian was a pretty thing who chewed on a pencil eraser from time to time, sticking the pencil in her mouth the way you would a cigarette.

I found a long table to sit at and looked through the campus books, picked out the ones on East Texas, and started there. It said what the tuition was and what kind of campus housing they had, and an idea of what it would cost if you lived off campus.

Melinda would prefer off campus, so I looked at that first. When I got through looking at the prices for tuition, books—which was estimated, depending on classes—and housing, it was quite a bit.

I looked then at the on-campus housing. It was only marginally better, but if I put down a payment, paid the rest out by the semester, had the drive-in going, maybe buried a few dogs (and I intended to bury them for real), I could probably afford it.

Course, to do it the way I wanted to do it, me and Nancy would have to get married, so I'd have direct access, just in case she decided to lord it over me. That was a funny thing to think about a woman I was willing to kill for, but I wasn't fooling myself any. The businesses were a big part of it, and Nancy was no angel.

I decided Kilgore College might be the best bet. It was close by and I could see Melinda pretty often. When it came to registration, no one would know her father was black, because I knew someone who could fix the birth certificate if she needed it, and I presumed she would. For a hundred dollars, he had made my certificate white as snow. The man who fixed it was dark as coal and called himself my cousin on account of he knew I was not pure white. He thought it was funny. His hand was steady and he had the equipment to make it look just right. He was also someone I trusted, a friend, because when I was having the certificate redone, we ended up visiting, found that we liked each other. From time to time I went there to see him, there being on the dark side of town, as he called it. I went there and we drank beer and talked. He never came to see me. Where I lived wasn't fancy, but it was the white side of town, and for him to come there, well, it just wouldn't look right.

I brought all the books back, asked the librarian if she knew a way I could find out about places where a drunk could dry out. I told her I had a friend.

She thought a bit, put a pencil in her mouth and chewed on the eraser some more, then went and found me a big book with all manner of listings and addresses in it.

I found one in Dallas for drying out. They called it something fancy, but it was really a drunk farm. It was expensive, but again, I thought about the money. Nancy had told me how much the insurance policy was for, and death by accident doubled it. It was a lot. Just a piece of it, a small piece, could send Melinda to college and my mama to that place to dry out.

I might even get Mama a real house with a white picket fence and dog in the yard. Hire someone to do windows, shovel up the dog shit, and mow the lawn.

Yeah. I was starting to see myself as living the kind of life my father never could have. It wouldn't have mattered what kind of brains he had, a black man in the South, it wasn't going to happen. And up north, my brother, well, he was still a black man, and he could do all right, but he'd always do what a black man could do, not what a white man could.

(26)

When I knew Melinda would be close to getting off work, I drove over to Mama's house trailer and got out and walked up to the door. I could hear the air conditioner running. I knocked. It took a long time for Mom to answer. When she opened the door, she smiled.

"Baby boy," she said. "Come in."

I went inside and we embraced. "Thought I'd come before Melinda got home, see you, and then I'm going to try and talk my little sister into going to get ice cream. I can bring you something back." I said it that way to cut off any possibility she might be entertaining the idea of going with us. I didn't want her to. I wanted to visit with Melinda alone. Besides, unless there was liquor involved, Mama seldom went out.

She pursed her lips and thought for a moment. "Well, some chocolate. Two scoops of anything as long as one of them is chocolate."

"Cones don't survive long drives. How about I get you a pint of something, chocolate something or another."

"That sounds good. I don't mind if it's got pecans in it or some kind of nut."

Her hands were shaking, but I thought her complexion looked better than last time. She hadn't combed her hair in a few days and she was wearing a loose muumuu that made her look a little like an animal poking its head out of the top of a tent, but she was certainly steady-enough-looking. She had on pink house shoes and was carrying a pack of cigarettes in one hand and a box of kitchen matches in the other. She walked into the kitchen, set the matches and cigarettes on the kitchen table, and put on the coffeepot. "You got time for a cup, right?"

"Sure. Listen, Mama. I think I might be working on a deal that could get me better off and, in turn, make you and Melinda better off."

She looked at me out of the corner of her eye. "How much better off?"

"A lot."

"What you got in mind?"

"Can't say right now, just in case it falls through. But it could be like you want, me making some real money."

"I see," she said. I couldn't figure if she was happy her life-long dream of seeing me embrace whiteness and big money might happen or if she was thinking what she might do with that money. I voted on the latter.

I don't know why I bothered to try and please her. It was like I had some kind of twitch I couldn't prevent.

We sat in chairs at the kitchen and waited on the coffee.

"I think that's great. Can you tell me anything?"

"Not really, but it looks good."

"I married your father because I thought he was the handsomest man I ever saw. Big and strong. Masculine. But he had a temper, and him being colored, well, I put a brand on myself, and he had limitations financially. When we split, and I moved here, I thought I could do better, but I couldn't. I was on the drink, you know?"

She said that like I might have no idea.

The coffee got ready and we had a cup. Mama told me Melinda was thinking they might brighten the place up with new curtains and better lighting.

The only thing that could brighten up that shit hole was a house fire.

I got up and poured us another cup of coffee, sat down with it, put her cup in front of her. She looked into it as if its contents might contain prophecy, like she was divining chicken guts or reading lines in a person's palm.

Mama, carefully, as if there was some special technique about it, pulled a cigarette from the pack on the table, put it in her mouth, pushed the matchbox open, and took out a match. She struck the match on the strike strip and lit her cigarette. She shook out the match and dropped it into a piled ashtray on the table.

She took a deep puff, pulling the smoke inside of her. When she let it out, she said, "I had such high hopes for you."

Shit. Now it was coming. It was like that coffee was alcohol all of a sudden, not some hot, sobering cup of caffeine. I guess it's what you might call a dry drunk. Whatever was wrong with her, it came in waves, and this was the start of one of those waves. Her face changed and her eyes seemed to darken.

"Just said I had something good about to happen."

"But you won't tell me what it is, so I got to figure it's just talk. What? You might get promoted to service manager at the car lot? That it? An extra fifty dollars a month take-home pay?"

"Come on, Mama."

"You come on. You need to make something big of yourself. Not get promoted at the car lot."

"I never said that's what I had in mind."

"Got a new job at the post-oak plant, putting creosote on posts? Driving a goddamn forklift?"

I heard Melinda drive up.

"I'm doing my best," I said.

"Your best seems wanting, don't it?"

I didn't know what to say. She was looking at me with a hard face and a set of eyes that looked charred. I barely recognized her. I stood up from the table as Melinda came in the front door. I could see her through the open door of the kitchen.

"Hey, Eddie," she said.

"Hey, baby sister. Me and Mama were just talking about my bright future."

Melinda studied us, and she got the deal right away. With her living there, she must have seen Mama's dry drunk more than a time or two.

"Yeah, she talks about mine too, but making good for a girl. You know, fucking my way to the top of the pile."

"You don't need to talk like that," Mama said.

"I'm going to find some old man with money who has one foot in a bear trap and the other on a banana peel, and I'm going to push him down so he can't get back up, and then I'll inherit his money."

Mama had turned in the chair to look at Melinda, who had come into the kitchen and was leaning against the door frame.

"That's silly."

"But it's in the ballpark," Melinda said. "You want us to make it so you can make it, like our big brother has, who sends you some money every month. Money you spend on getting drunk and smoking cigarettes. It isn't about seeing us do well, it's about seeing you do well."

Mama stood up, picked up her cigarettes and matches. "Neither of you are like your brother. You're both losers."

"And him being the full-on nigger and all," Melinda said.

Mama started toward her. I thought she might knock Melinda

out of the way, but Melinda stepped aside, and, moving faster than I had seen her move in a long time, Mama went on down the hall toward her bedroom.

"A family get-together is so refreshing to the spirit, don't you think?" Melinda said.

"Would you like to go for ice cream?"

"I'd like to go for anything and anywhere, just as long as it's away from here."

(27)

I asked if we could go in her car and if she would let me drive. Where I was hoping we'd end up after the ice cream, I didn't want a big, bright, memorable Cadillac parked there.

When we got inside her car, we both let out our breath, like we had been underwater for a while. I started the car and drove us out of there.

"I guess it was the lack of alcohol talking back there," Melinda said, "but I tell you, big brother, I am tired of it. I say let her drink. I say I get out of the house and she can live on the money my other big brother sends her, which, for the record, isn't that much and not that often. I bet if he was here, she'd be riding his ass. Hell, he's my brother, and I would barely recognize him if he came through the door with his name on a sign hung around his neck."

"We kind of got separated."

"Mama separated us. She wanted to move here and start over, and she did. But starting over for her was a lot like not starting over, just doing what she'd done all along someplace else. Hell, she's worse. At least when she and Daddy used to fight, they'd end up in bed. You could hear them through the walls in there, screwing like rabid weasels, the springs squeaking like a bunch of mice."

"I remember, and I'd rather not."

"Everyone likes a roll in the sheets, big brother. Even your father and mother. Even me."

"Jesus, don't talk to me about that. You're a kid."

"I have a birthday next month. I'll be twenty."

"Shit, really?"

"Yeah. Thanks for keeping up with my birthdays."

I drove us to the drugstore. They sold ice cream there, but not in pints. We'd have to drop by a grocery store to get that for Mama. I ought to have just sent her back my best wishes, but I knew I wouldn't.

Before we got out of the car, Melinda said, "You know, people here knew we had a drop of colored in us, they wouldn't let us through those doors."

"I know. And sometimes I feel like an impostor, and other times I feel like 'Fuck all of you. I got the sneaky edge on you.'"

"I feel like I'd like to have something vanilla with chocolate topping."

Inside we ordered up what we wanted, and I paid and they handed it over the counter to us. Two cones. Vanilla with chocolate topping and, for me, plain vanilla.

We sat at a table and began to eat the ice cream.

I said, "You know, I thought we'd have an ice cream, but I want to do something else."

"Yeah?"

"I think I'm coming into some money."

"We're out of rich relatives who might die and send us some dough. Mom's people disowned her, and Daddy's people, except for our big brother, will die owing money."

"It's another thing."

"What kind of thing?"

"I want to find out before I tell you, but I wanted to do something just in case, while I have a bit of car-sale money in my pocket."

"You always have car-sale money. You're doing all right, Eddie. You don't need to keep trying to be Rockefeller."

"I want to get your birth certificate altered."

Melinda thought about that. "You mean take out the colored-daddy part."

I nodded. "I did it for mine. Sometimes, something comes up, you have to show a birth certificate, and, well . . ."

"Looks better if it's all white?"

"Exactly. And listen, you want to go to college, that could come up. They don't dig much beyond that."

"We been over this."

"Yeah, but now I'm talking having the money to send you somewhere like Kilgore College, plus enough to get Mama dried out. There's a place in Dallas."

"You got a lot worked out on a maybe."

"I know, but we ought to get some things done. It would be better if we did."

"And how do I do this, get a fake birth certificate?"

"It's made to look like the original only we change one word. The place where it says 'race.'"

"You put in 'white' instead of 'colored.'"

"That's it."

"I don't know how I feel about that, Eddie."

"Let me do this for you. I got money for it, and this other deal I got planned goes through, there'll be enough for the other things."

Melinda sat and thought and licked at her ice cream cone. She looked small then, and I was reminded of when we were kids. I knew to wait and say nothing. I'd had experience. You pushed her, she'd lock up like a safe.

She didn't seem all that happy about it, but she said, "Okay. I guess so. Okay."

(28)

When we walked out to the car, a redheaded teenager standing on the corner whistled at Melinda.

"You best put that whistle in your pocket," I said, "and keep it there."

The teenager turned, walked down the block and turned a corner and was gone.

"I thought he was kind of cute," Melinda said.

"You would."

We drove over the railroad tracks and went along a narrow street, through the colored part of town, the biggest part of it, and on out in the country a bit to where there was a nice white house with a nice white Chrysler in the driveway. Out back there was an aluminum garage with one window cut into it, and an air conditioner was set in that window. When we got out of the car, we could hear the air conditioner humming along.

I knocked on the door of the house. No one answered.

"So we made the trip for nothing?" Melinda said.

"Car's here. He's here. Probably out back."

We went out to the aluminum building, and I knocked on that

door. There was a little peephole in the door, and though I couldn't know for sure, a few seconds after I knocked, I had the sensation of being watched through it.

A moment later I heard a lock snick, and the door opened. Dash, who had a face that looked to have seen a bit of this and that and felt amused by all of it, was standing there. His processed hair was whipped back in a Little Richard pompadour, and he had on a white shirt and suspenders holding up his tan slacks. He had on tan shoes. He looked like he was dressed up to go to a party. He always looked that way, even if the bulk of his day was spent drinking beer and going to shit.

"Damn, man," Dash said, smiling big, showing us that one of his front teeth was gold and had a silver star in it. "You got one fine woman with you."

"That's my sister."

"Oh, man, I didn't mean no disrespect. But damn."

"May we come in?"

"I suppose you can."

Dash moved from the door and walked through the building, which was nice inside. It had a thin wooden partition at the back, a big couch, and a TV set with rabbit ears on it, each of them topped with aluminum foil, and there was a refrigerator against the wall on the opposite side. There were soft lights.

Behind that partition, I knew, he had a camera for making false documents, a printing press, inks and pens and special paper.

Dash stopped at the refrigerator, reached in, and pulled out a bottle of beer. "Y'all want a cold beer?"

"That's all right," I said.

"I'd like one," Melinda said.

"No, she wouldn't," I said.

"I'm old enough," she said.

"No, you're not."

"Well," Dash said, "I'm having one, and some peanuts with it."

He went over to the couch and sat down, used a church key resting on the end table to open his beer, and took a swig. There were peanuts in a bowl on the end table. He reached out, picked up a few, and popped them into his mouth.

"Way you act," he said, studying me in that way he had, a way that always made you think he knew more than you, "I got to figure you aren't here on a social visit. I'm going to guess you need me to fix her up a birth certificate."

"That's right."

"And the only thing you need special is for me to make her father white. You got the dough?"

"No. I'm going to trade you some chickens for it."

"Here's the thing. I've gone up. Ink has gotten more expensive."

"I doubt that."

"Then let's say it's the paper. Or, better yet, it's going to cost you because I know you need it, and I'm a goddamn artist. Damn, man, you sure that's your sister?"

"I'm sure, and you better be too."

"You ain't going to rough me up like you done Cecil, are you?"

"You know about that?"

"Who don't on this end of town? He looked like he'd been tenderized with a mallet and then run over with a truck. Keep in mind a guy like that, he's going to remember you. And, damn, girl. I'm not trying to be rude, but you are movie-star quality."

"Is that one of your lines you give women?" Melinda said, but I could tell she liked it.

"It is, but mostly with the others it's a lie."

"You are slick," she said.

"I'm all kinds of things."

"You're also too old for me."

"Man, just because I have snow on the roof don't mean I ain't got a fire in the furnace."

"You don't have snow on your roof."

"I dye it."

"Look, we're going to give you the information," I said, deciding to have a beer from the refrigerator, pulling one out for Melinda too, "then we'll leave you to it."

"You think I'm doing it this afternoon? I got other documents in line to forge. You think you can skip in the queue?"

I used the church key that was on the end table to open our beers. "Just one beer, baby sis. You've seen what this stuff can do to a person."

"Just one," she said. "And by the way, big brother, you think this is my first one?"

I had second thoughts, but I gave her the beer. I said to Dash, "I'll put a big bill on top of what you want if you can get right to it."

Dash thought about that for about two seconds. "How big a bill?"

"Big enough."

"That case, I'm thinking some of these others can wait. I got a couple fake marriage certificates, a death certificate for someone that ain't dead, but I can jump over that shit, way you're stacking up the greenbacks. That there will move you ahead in line."

"How much ahead?"

"About a week, you want it to look right when you hold it up to the light. If I do it the way it's supposed to be done, and I will, then that damn thing is your birth certificate. You got her original birth certificate?"

"I don't. But we give you the information, you can make it from scratch, same as mine."

"You know your original is registered?"

"It's just for show."

"Like I said, no one will be able to tell which one is real and which one isn't. You show one I make around, it'll do the job, I guarantee."

"That's what I want. So, Cecil's telling about how I clipped him. What kind of shit is he spreading?"

"Well, he's just mad over the ass-whipping. He don't know you got the nigger connection, I don't think. Depends on what your mama told him."

"She's not proud of it, so I doubt she said anything, and don't say that."

"Say what?"

"You know what."

He grinned at me, flashing that gold tooth with the silver star. "Listen here, Ed, those people play cards and such out at the country house, they don't fuck around. They're some bad dudes. They ain't civilized like you and me."

"They didn't seem that bad to me."

"You caught them good, all right, but maybe they wasn't expecting much. Now it could get all exciting, like. Cecil, he don't take good to being embarrassed and disrespected in front of friends."

"I wanted to make an impression."

"You did. Look here, Ed. You're tough with a blackjack and a pistol, and I got to admire the balls you got on you—pardon me, miss—but guys like Cecil, they just looking to let the air out of them big balls of yours, make them go flat.

"Listen up, man. Know you got to take care of your mama, and I don't blame you for wanting you and your sister to pass. If I wasn't so black my shadow looked pale, I'd take advantage of that shit too, though the world would lose one handsome black son of a bitch. But I'm telling you—be on the lookout."

"Thanks for the tip."

"Jesus, Eddie," Melinda said. "This sounds dangerous. I told you that wasn't a good thing to do."

"I'm fine."

"I was thinking about me," she said. "Maybe he'll have something against me. I drove you out there that night."

"Yeah, but he don't know that," I said and looked at Dash. "About the birth certificate?"

Dash swigged the last of his beer and revealed his shiny white teeth. "Show me the money, my man. Show me the money."

(29)

We went by the Piggly Wiggly and bought Mama some ice cream and then I drove Melinda home.

Before she got out of the car, I said, "I'll get that certificate to you."

"This is making me nervous. You rushing this birth-certificate thing, trying to get me and Mama moved off, and you talking about some kind of vague plan about money."

"It's all good, sis. Take Mama her ice cream, and you'll hear from me soon enough."

We got out and I climbed in my Cadillac and drove home. When I got there, I spread the tarp in the bathroom and started painting the walls with my new brushes and paint.

I finished, washed up a little, left the tarp lying there. I had deliberately splashed some paint on it, though I managed to get plenty on it in the process of painting. Drunk chimpanzees could have done as good a job as I did. I doubted I would ever need to worry about it, but if I did, the tarp would actually have paint that matched the stuff I had left in the cans. I was going to put them in the storeroom under the outside stairs.

I fixed myself a cup of coffee, making it a little heavy on water and light on coffee, then sat down on the couch and read a stack of magazines. I was thinking about Nancy, how she was doing, when the phone rang, and it was her.

"He's gone," she said. "Probably on his sixth beer by now. Time he comes home, if you could squeeze the beer out of him, it would fill the bathtub. Do I really have to wait for him to come home? I'm not liking how that might go."

"Just stay the course," I said. "We have to do it there, set it up at the creek. I got some of the stuff we need. You got bleach?"

"Why?"

"You got any?"

"Yeah, but again, why?"

"Well, you need to have that and plenty of throwaway rags tomorrow night because that's when we get him. And it will be messy. You hear me?"

"I hear you, and I'll get what's needed." She sounded as if suddenly she were out of breath.

"You want to turn back, and frankly, I'm thinking you might want to, this is the time."

"What about you?"

"I've dealt myself in."

"Then we're set. Why don't we do it tonight?"

"You'll need those rags and bleach. And I have to get my head right to do this. I've got everything set I know how to set, and now it's my head I have to set. I'll be ready tomorrow night. You call me when he goes off to drink."

"Ed, you sure about all this, doing it so we get away with it?"

"I don't know you can be sure about that kind of thing, but I'm thinking it through. I wouldn't take a crack at this, I didn't believe we had a chance to get away with it. Do the best with him tonight you can, and tomorrow we end this. And then there's just you and me and the future, baby."

(30)

I worried all night long and sometimes felt a little sick. I was going to beat a man to death with a crowbar. I knew how I would feel afterward—worse than with that Korean, and that was bad enough—but I was committed. I kept focusing on Nancy and the drive-in and that little pet cemetery. My American dream, drenched in blood and greed, but I didn't care. I wanted what I wanted.

Next day I went to work, and hardly anyone came to the lot, and those that did weren't thinking about buying. They had just come to look. You get so you can tell right away.

About an hour before I was supposed to get off, I was in the car-lot garage, putting air in the tires on a Ford, when Dave came waddling in.

"Finish up the air in those tires, go on home, Ed. Day's dead as Old Yeller."

"All right," I said. I finished up airing the tires and drove home. I got the tarp wrapped up tight, making a reasonably small package, and slipped it inside the two plastic laundry bags, one bag pushed down inside the other, and then the tarp inside of that. I had the crowbar in the car already, along with some electrician tape, so I carried the bags with the tarp inside of them out to the car and put them in the trunk. I did it carefully, making sure no one was watching me.

I went back upstairs and tried to watch some TV, waiting on Nancy's call, and it came about eight.

"He's gone. Come now. I want to get this done."

I packed an extra pair of clothes in a grip and drove over to Nancy's. There was that bumpy gravel trail that ran past the animal cemetery, and I used that and parked the Cadillac behind the garage. Frank pulled in the way he always did, the good path to the garage, he'd never see the Cadillac.

When I got that done, I pulled the tarp and crowbar out of the trunk and got hold of the grip with the clothes in it and walked up to the back door of the house. I didn't even have time to knock. Nancy opened it. She'd been watching for me.

Inside, I dropped the tarp, crowbar, and grip, and she fell into my arms and I kissed her. The light in the kitchen was off, so it wasn't until I was inside, in the bedroom and she had closed the blinds that she turned on the light and I saw her face.

She was wearing a faded blue nightgown and was beat up worse than the night before. I felt guilty then for waiting, but it had been the right thing to do. I was worked up now, like I was going to charge a hill against a lot of Koreans.

"Damn, girl."

"He knocked me plumb out, and I woke up in real pain. He was doing things to me he hadn't done before . . . and, well, I bled."

"Jesus," I said. "Well, that shit ends tonight."

We pulled the tarp out of the bags and placed it over the bed to protect the mattress. The paint side was up and the paint had dried. I pushed the bags under the bed where I could reach them.

I climbed on the bed and stood on it while I took the lightbulb out of the socket. I got down from there and put the bulb in the nightstand drawer That way, he came in, he wouldn't see the tarp on the bed, and it would maybe give me some shadow cover when I came out of the closet with the crowbar.

"I would make love to you, Ed, but I'm hurt all over."

"That's all right. I'm not feeling all that romantic."

"I'm kind of excited."

"Thing like this, it won't be pretty."

"I'm still ready."

I couldn't see her face there in the dark, but I felt like I could feel the excitement coming off of her in warm waves. Truth was, I felt a little bit that way myself.

"All right, then," I said.

(31)

I checked out the closet and pushed some of the clothes on the rack to one side and made sure I could squeeze in there. I took the crowbar in there with me along with my grip with the spare clothes in it and pulled the door closed after I put some of the black electrician tape over the part of the door that stuck into the frame. I wanted to be able to push it open easy and not have the snicking sound of the lock and the doorjamb connection. I tried it a few times. It seemed fine.

I opened up the closet and stepped out with the crowbar in my hand.

"Is that heavy?" Nancy said.

"Heavy enough."

"Should I fix coffee? I mean, I don't know exactly what you do when you're waiting to murder somebody."

"You got anything to eat? I haven't eaten." I had been so worked up about getting worked up to do what needed to be done, I had forgotten to eat. All of a sudden, I was starving.

Nancy fixed me a sandwich with bologna and cheese and made coffee. When that was done, she turned out the light and we sat at the kitchen table.

"Which door does he come in?"

"Always this one. From the back into the kitchen, way you came."

"All right. And he goes straight to bed?"

"Pretty much."

"What's 'pretty much' mean?"

"Sometimes he goes to the bathroom to pee. Sometimes he likes to get the beating started right away."

"What I want you to be prepared for, is when I come out of that closet, you need to get out of the way, because I'm going to be swinging for the fence, and you don't want to get in front of it. You got those beer cans I asked you to save?"

"They're in a black trash bag in the garage. He'll park his car there. I left it open."

"I saw. I'm parked behind it."

"What else?"

"Fishing gear?"

"Tackle box and rods, they're out there and ready to be put in his car. Anything else?"

"I think beating him to death with a crowbar and taking him out to the creek and making his murder look like an accident is plenty for one night."

"Ed, I know how horrible this is, but he has to go. It's not as if his life matters much."

"He have living parents?"

"A mother in Tulsa, but he never sees her."

"Still, it might matter to her."

"I don't want to think about that, that someone might miss him."

"Then don't."

"Let's think about the insurance money, about how you and I can run the businesses better than Frank."

"Then that's what we'll think about, but what shall we talk about?"

"Small talk seems out of place."

"It does. I think we should have another cup of coffee. We got a long night ahead of us."

(32)

About two in the morning headlights swept across the backyard, moved down the gravel drive toward the open garage.

I had drunk about five cups of coffee, and I was wide awake and my skin itched with caffeine. I couldn't have gone to sleep short of death. Saw those lights, I wanted to change my mind, just get up and walk out the front door and hide somewhere, sneak around to my car later.

But I didn't.

"What now?" Nancy said.

"You know what now."

I went into the bedroom with her.

She took off her robe. She had a slip on under it. She climbed onto the bed. "I'm so scared, Ed."

"So am I." I lifted the blinds and looked out. I could see his car's taillights in the garage. I faintly heard his car door slam, and then I saw a hulk of shadow, and then the hulk came out of the garage, and the little light over the garage doors shone down on him.

He was damn big. Bigger than I'd expected, and his shoulders were wide and thick. He kind of wandered all over the place, went down on one knee once and managed to get himself up, which was like watching an erector set being constructed.

Good. Him being drunk would work to my advantage.

I watched until he was about halfway to the kitchen door, then I said, "Showtime, baby."

I got in the closet with the crowbar and gently closed the door. The closet seemed tighter than before, and I started sweating. There was a feeling in my ears like you get from altitude, and my mouth was dry and coppery-tasting. I was gripping the crowbar so tight, my hand started to hurt. I switched it to my other hand, then back again. I tried to take control of my breathing. My heart was beating fast enough, I thought it was going to break through my chest.

I remembered that we hadn't removed the bulb from the lamp, so if he turned that on, he'd see the tarp. Okay, I told myself, that won't matter, because I'm going to be on him like skin cells in a couple of seconds.

I heard the kitchen screen door open, then the door. The screen slammed and then the door slammed. Frank sounded like he carried his own china shop with him, the noise he made.

"Nancy," he called out, and then again, "Nancy."

Nancy said, "I'm in here, Frank."

"I think I need some more of what I had last night." His voice was louder now.

"I don't want to, Frank."

"I didn't ask what you wanted," he said. His words were understandable but slurred. "I'm thinking I get a little of that back-door stuff again."

I gently pushed the door, cracked it open a little. I could see Nancy's shape on the bed. She was on her knees in the center of it.

Frank came into view, took off his hat and flung it, and started taking off his pants at the edge of the bed. He was having trouble, he was so drunk. Good Lord, he was big enough to hunt tigers with nothing but a bad attitude.

I eased the closet door open wider, stepped out as Frank said, "What's this thing on the bed?"

That's when I sort of skipped across the room and swung the crowbar.

The swing was brutal. It made a little whistling sound when I swung it. The bar caught him in the back of the head with a smack like someone snapping a fresh cracker. He stumbled, and with his pants down around his ankles, he tripped and landed on the floor by the side of the bed.

He threw one hand to the back of his head as he got up. He did it quick for a drunk. It was like the blow, instead of knocking him flat, had merely sobered him up. His pants were still around his ankles.

That's when I hit him again, but this time he was turning, and I caught him across the face. I felt a wet splash on my cheek, and something hard hit me there. Frank fell backward and his feet popped up with his pants still around them.

Nancy had slipped off the bed and was on the opposite side of it, easing back toward the wall.

Frank let out with what sounded like a wild-animal growl, sat up, and tried kicking his pants off his shoes but couldn't manage it. I stepped in to hit him again, aiming for the top of his head, but he reached out and snatched the nightstand by the bed up. The lamp on it hit the floor and broke into pieces, and my blow hit the top of the nightstand he used to shield himself.

I started swinging desperately, but all I could hit was that nightstand. With his pants around his ankles, he stood up, holding that nightstand. When he called out, it was loud. "What have you done, Nancy?"

I tell you, he wasn't drunk anymore. Not even in the least. He swung the nightstand at me the same time I was swinging the crow-bar, and they came together and the nightstand came apart in some large splinters. The contact was so hard, it knocked me down.

Lying on my back I looked up, and he leaned down to grab me, so me and my crowbar rolled under the bed, and I started crawling to the other side.

I glanced back, saw that where his feet had been, there were only the pants. He had managed to work his way out of them. I felt pressure on the bed, the springs and mattress pushing down on me, but I crawled and came out on the other side just as he stepped off the bed, wearing shoes, boxers, and his shirt, the shirttails dangling. He grabbed Nancy by the throat. "You bitch," he said.

I caught him with the crowbar on the back of his right leg. He let go of Nancy, went down on his knees, and I swung with everything I had for his head. In that moment, the world slowed down, and it was as if I could see shadows moving in the room, a bit of light slipping through the blinds on the far wall. The crowbar whistled, but it seemed to me I was hung in time and that it would never get to its destination. Frank was turning, and that's when I caught him high on the forehead and there was a sound much stronger than a broken fresh cracker. It was like someone had snapped off a rifle shot, the way it sounded. Frank's head flew back and popped forward again. I had swung so hard that when I hit him, it knocked me down, but that big bastard was still on his knees.

As I was trying to get up, he reached out and got me by the throat, and damn if he wasn't slowly standing up and lifting me with him.

I still had the crowbar and Nancy had grabbed him around his bare legs, was trying to bring him down, but she might as well have been trying to push over a redwood tree.

I swung at him with the crowbar and got him along the side of the head, and that and my weight made him drop me.

I hit on my back and then he fell on top of me. I started scream-ing, it was so crazy, and then I realized he wasn't moving.

I pushed out from under him, got up, and hit him in the head with the crowbar again. I imagined he was that gook in Korea, and I had the rifle butt, and it was him or me, which in both cases it was.

Nancy crawled over the bed, leaned down, pulled the plastic bags from under it, crawled back, and gave them to me.

I dropped the crowbar, fitted the bags over his head, got my knees in his back, clenched the bags tight behind his neck, and pulled.

"Get that bulb, turn on the light." I didn't let loose of the twist in that bag, and I was pulling so hard I had lifted his head off the floor.

In the meantime, Nancy was scrambling about for the lightbulb. "It's broken," she said. "It was in the nightstand drawer."

"Well, get the one out of the lamp, put it in." I relaxed a little bit because Frank was no longer moving.

The bulb in the lamp had survived, and she stood on the bed and screwed it in where we had removed the other. She hurried over to the wall and turned on the light.

By now I had quit tugging and figured the air was out of him. He still wasn't moving. I couldn't feel a pulse. The room was bright and spinning a little.

I struggled to my feet and sat on the edge of the bed, and Nancy came over and sat by me. I glanced around. There was blood on the tarp, but most of it was on the wall and the floor, and when I looked up, I saw the ceiling was spattered with it. I looked at Nancy. She had blood on her face, and I could feel the blood on mine.

I said, "Listen. Go get those clean-up rags and the bleach."

She went and got them, and we went to work. It took a lot of time to wipe the walls, floor, and ceiling and make sure everything was bleached down.

When we finished, she took my grip out of the closet and sat it on the floor. She wiped off her face, and I wiped off mine, then we took off our clothes.

The idea was to shower, but we found ourselves clinging to each other, and then we were on the bed, and we weren't thinking about the tarp and the blood. We were thinking about savage satisfaction.

(33)

Getting his pants back on him was a struggle, and I had to take his shoes off to get them to pull up easier. Once I got the pants on him, I worked his shirttails into them, fastened his belt.

Meanwhile, Nancy was putting his shoes back on, tying them.

"All right, get his hat," I said. "I'm going to get his car, drive it around. We can load him in it on the passenger side, and I'll drive out to the bridge. You follow in your car. Got it?"

"I got it."

"I'll go slow, but not too slow. We don't want to look like we're in a hurry, but I don't want to be out there poking along so someone remembers me if they see me. This time of morning, not likely, I'm hoping. You follow a good pace back, not on my ass."

"Got it."

"I get out there, unlikely case someone is there, I'm going to just drive on, and you do the same, and we'll figure from there, on down the road a piece. You still with me?"

"I am."

"We get what we got to get done, we come back here and clean this place up again, just to be sure, make the bedroom look spotless. Then we want to air it out. Someone comes here, just to check, you know, and it could happen, we don't want the place smelling like bleach, making someone curious, so we use enough of that to get the job done, then we get a bit of cleaner to deodorize, something with a smell. You know, strawberry, vanilla, some such. I didn't think of that, but we get it tomorrow, we'll probably be all right."

"You didn't mention it, but I thought of it. I bought some stuff you can spray around."

"Good, you're ahead of me. We don't have what we need, we might have to buy it, but I think we can do it easy enough with what you got." I knew I was talking nervous, but I couldn't stop myself. "I'll take the tarp then and get rid of it. First, let's get it off the bed, make sure we don't get blood on the mattress."

"It's okay, Ed. We've done good."

"Yeah. I know."

We carefully folded and pulled the tarp off the mattress. I put it out in the yard by the side of the house. Back inside, I fished the car keys out of his front pants pocket, then I walked out to the garage and put the fishing gear into the car, in the back seat, opened one of the windows so the poles would poke out of it. I put his box of hooks and sinkers and the like on the floorboard behind the front passenger seat.

I pulled the car around behind the house, opened the front passenger door. Nancy helped me carry Frank out, me holding him under the shoulders, her holding his legs. He was a load. She dropped her end a couple of times, but we finally got him through the passenger door and into the seat. I had to put his hat on him again because it had fallen off. I set him up in the seat so if someone did see us, he'd look like he was riding.

It was still dark, but with the porch light on, I could see his face was really beat up. His nose was broken and his lip was busted.

"All right, make a sandwich," I said. "You got a thermos, make some coffee and fill it."

"So you're going to have a snack? Right now?"

"Going fishing, I figure he might take his lunch with him. We'll put it in the car, they look it over, they'll find the sandwich, the thermos."

"Of course. I get it. Sorry."

We went inside and she made the sandwich and I started some coffee. She found a thermos, and I filled it when the coffee was ready. She put the sandwich in a paper bag and I took the bag and thermos out to the car, put them on the floorboard behind the driver's seat.

"Now the beer cans."

Nancy went inside and came out with a large sack of them.

"Too many," I said. "I'll pour some on the floorboard."

I did that, and when I felt it was enough, I gave her the bag with the rest in it to take back inside.

When she came out again, she took hold of my arm. She had quite a grip.

"Now we do the other part," I said. "We get that done, I think we're home-free. After that, wait a month, and you ask about the insurance."

"That's a long time."

"But it's a smart time. Listen, this creek, it's in the woods, but it's not a long way from here as the crow flies, so it shouldn't take any time at all. Just drive careful."

"I understand, Ed, don't wear me out with details."

"Sorry. Yeah, you're right. I'm nervous."

"So am I. I never helped kill a man before."

"We were better at it than we should be," I said.

I got in Frank's car, and Nancy went up to the garage to get the one I had sold her. She pulled out and I started for the highway, going at what I thought was the right speed.

It was still dark out.

I looked in my rearview. I could see the lights from Nancy's car. She was following at just the right distance.

With the back window open, the wind whistled in, and it seemed pretty chill, though I might have felt that way because I had just beat a man with a crowbar and smothered him with a plastic bag. You don't do that and not feel anything. I comforted myself with the notion he wasn't someone that needed to be living, that he might have killed Nancy eventually.

I turned down a blacktop and drove for a bit, and then I took a clay road. I used to fish there, back when I fished. I had done a lot of that when I had first moved here with Mama and Melinda, after the war, before I started working at the car lot. It was a nice, quiet place, and I had never been there and had someone else show up. Not early mornings, anyway, which was when I liked to fish, getting out there just before daylight. Like today.

A short time later, I came to the bridge. It wasn't very long, and it was even more precarious than I remembered it. There were spots on the sides of the bridge where parts of the railing was missing. I parked in the middle of the bridge, left the lights on, got out, looked over the side. There was a bit of moonlight on the water, and I could see pretty well.

It was about twenty feet down. The water was deep there. There was a natural depression and there were bits of leaves and sticks floating in it, being carried along by a brisk current.

Nancy parked behind me, left her lights on. She got out and came around and looked down at the water. "Is it deep enough?"

"Deep enough he could drown in it, and shallow enough someone can see the car, which is what we want."

"What now?"

I didn't answer. I got back in his car and pointed it so that the nose was against the bridge, then I put it in park, got out, reached across the seat, and pulled Frank in front of the steering wheel. The slick upholstery made it pretty easy to move him. I rolled down the driver's-side window. I closed the door. Nancy came over and took my arm.

"I'm going to reach in, pop the gear into drive, and it'll be enough to send it over. That railing would break if a butterfly flew into it. Best stand back."

I leaned in the window, got hold of the shift, and worked it into drive. The car rolled gently and then stopped against the railing.

Nancy put her hands on her hips. "You meant a big fucking butterfly, right?"

"I got it."

I went to the back of the car and pushed. This time it went through the rail, and it went quickly, and when it got to the rear wheels, it dropped, and hung on the bridge for a moment, then vibrated off. The car went into the water hood-first.

I looked at it. Its nose was on the bottom, and the rear end was sticking up in such a way you could clearly read the license plate.

I lifted my head and took a deep gulp of air.

Nancy said, "Oh, shit, Ed."

I looked down.

Frank was thrashing around in the water. He had come out of the window, and he was still alive, the cold water having rejuvenated what we thought was a dead body.

(34)

"He's fucking Rasputin," I said.

I didn't have the crowbar with me, but I edged down the end of the bridge, along the sloping dirt there, and when I got near the creek, I saw Frank had managed to put both hands on the bank and was trying to pull himself onto land. He wasn't moving so good, but I was surprised he was moving at all.

I found a large rock and picked that up. I went over and bent down over him and hit him in the head a couple of times so hard, my whole body vibrated. He let go of the dirt and slid back into the water, turning on his side, then on his back, and the current moved him. He went past the car and sailed like a big boat along the creek until it grew shallow, and then he washed up in a gravel bed next to the creek on the far side and lay there, his feet floating in the water where his legs stuck off into it.

I climbed back up the bank.

Nancy said, "Is he dead?"

"He's got to be," I said.

"How will it look now? He was already pretty beat up. Is anyone going to think he was killed by running off the bridge?"

"Banged around by the car, floated out the window, knocked

around by the rocks in the creek. A few days go by and they don't find him, well, birds and animals, what have you, will have been at work on him. Bunch of yokel cops and the like around here, I don't think they're going to think much about it. They like to solve their cases quick. They'll put 'accidental death' down fast so they can maybe go out and get to beating someone with a rubber hose."

Nancy drove us back, and inside we set to work cleaning again. It took several hours, and I found what had hit me in the cheek: one of Frank's teeth.

I put that in the commode and flushed it down. We bagged the bloody clean-up rags, and I took them outside and wrapped them up in the tarp. I would separate those, burn them somewhere, drop the tarp in the trash can, let it go to the dump.

When it was all done, we took a shower together, made love in the shower, and then we dried and dressed, me in the spare clothes I'd brought with me in the grip, Nancy in shorts and a sweatshirt. I had even cleaned the blood off the bottoms of my shoes.

I felt good about things.

We kissed, and I went to my car, carrying the crowbar, the tarp with the rags inside, and my grip with the bloody clothes in it.

I put all of that in the trunk of the Cadillac and was about to leave when I saw something stumbling around in the dark, carrying what looked like a small tree that had been pulled up by the roots, using it like a crude crutch. It was coming down the little road I had driven on, and as I watched, it cut away from that and crossed a patch of grass in front of the cemetery, heading toward Nancy's house.

It was Frank.

He wasn't Rasputin. He was the goddamn Frankenstein monster.

I got the pistol out of the glove box and decided I had no choice, that the whole plan had gone to hell, and I had to shoot him. And then I decided against it. I put my pistol in my waistband and got the crowbar out of the trunk again and hurried to Nancy's house.

I heard Nancy scream as she was standing at the back door, the screen closed. She'd been watching me from there, and now Frank had shown up. He was on the back steps, tugging at the screen door.

I ran up behind him, and when I was almost on him, he turned. His face was swollen and black in spots. One eye was closed, his nose was splayed sideways on his face, and part of his lip was dangling.

He made a grunting noise, opening his mouth enough I could see his tongue was black and he was missing some teeth.

He swung at me with that small tree, which actually proved to be a large limb. But he was weak. Why wouldn't he be? He had been hit repeatedly with a crowbar, smothered, run off a bridge into water, cracked on the head with a rock, and left to die, and still he had enough in him to find a stick and make it home to even the score.

He was so weak that the limb hit me and it was like being brushed with a feather. But I was doing all right. I hit him hard right in the center of the head. He fell down face-first in the yard. I thought I might get a saw and cut his head off, just to make sure, but I still believed the plan might work.

I lifted his head and peered into his one open eye. It had a glaze over it, and the pupil was as still as a thumbtack in a white board.

Nancy came outside. "Is he . . . finally dead?"

"Goddamn, I hope so. I don't know how much more I got in me. I'm going to change clothes and take him back to the creek."

I did just that, putting on the bloody ones again. Nancy rode out there with me. The sun was coming up when I dragged him out of the trunk and flipped his big ass over the side of the bridge. He hit the back of the car and fell into the water and went under. We watched for a while to see if he would swim up.

He didn't.

"Finally," Nancy said.

We went back to the house and I changed quickly, gave Nancy a kiss, told her to call me when she could, and drove home.

(35)

When I got home, I separated the rags from the tarp and put them in the grip with my bloody clothes. I put the tarp in the trash can and put it out on the curb. That very morning was trash day.

I kept the grip. I was going to burn that or maybe take it out in the country and bury it. I washed the crowbar off in the tub. It was caked with dried blood and brains. I watched the blood run down the drain. I barely made it to the toilet. I threw up everything inside of me, and then it was the dry heaves. I thought it would never stop.

I was so tired I almost called in sick to work, but I didn't think that was a good idea, so I spruced up a little more, combed my hair, brushed my teeth, used a lot of mouthwash to get the vomit smell out of my mouth, put some eye water in my eyes, and decided that I had better have breakfast and some coffee.

I hardly ate any of it, and the coffee made my stomach churn.

I took the crowbar out with me and unlocked the shed under the stairs and put the crowbar in it.

At work, I came into the office, and Dave looked up. "Man, son, you look like you been wrestling a bear."

I kind of had been. "Slept bad. One of those nights."

"I'd tell you to go home, but I need you here because I have a doctor's appointment today."

I decided I'd try coffee again, so I poured some from the pot setting on the hot plate and put more sugar in it than I usually did.

I sat down at my desk and Dave talked the way he always talked, but today I didn't want to hear it. I pretended things couldn't be better, smiled and nodded a lot.

I managed to drink the coffee, and he got up to go to his appointment.

"Nothing serious, I hope."

"Doctor just likes to check me over once a year. Had a few heart episodes. No attacks, but some episodes. Mostly, though, it's just a general look-over. Between you and me, I think he likes to poke his finger up my ass."

"Who wouldn't?"

Dave cackled and left.

I sat there and sipped the coffee and it managed to rest comfortably enough in my stomach. I replayed last night over and over in my head. The way the crowbar made that sound against his skull, him with his pants down and me swinging away, crawling under the bed. The way he came out of the water and I had to use the rock on him. The way he came walking back to the house, probably with only a brain cell or two left, and then us taking him out there again and dropping him over the bridge and him landing on his car and rolling off in the water and sinking under.

He had to have come up by now and started floating a bit, though the creek got shallow beyond the deep hole, so he would be visible in the water. I hoped the buzzards would do their work. But then again, for Nancy to get the money, they had to find enough of him to know who he was.

No one drove onto the lot for even a look that morning, and

around noon, I locked up the office and went over to a hamburger place and had a cheeseburger, fries, and a Coke. I could eat the burger, but I wasn't ready for the greasy fries. The Coke seemed to help settle my stomach.

Jesus Christ, what had I done?

I had to take comfort in knowing he wouldn't be hitting Nancy and raping her anymore. I had to take comfort in that, but right then, sitting there in the booth with half a hamburger and a pile of oily fries in front of me, there wasn't a lot of comfort to be had.

To make myself feel better, I thought about the insurance money, the drive-in, the animal cemetery, and I thought about Nancy, how soft and warm she was. I thought about that as much as I could so as not to think about the other.

Mama wouldn't like what I'd had to do to get that money, but the idea of me owning a business, even partly owning it, would be something that would impress her. In a year, I'd be doing better than my brother.

When I got back to work, Dave was still out, and I'd no sooner unlocked the office than a car drove onto the lot. It was a colored couple.

There was an unwritten Dave rule that you didn't sell to colored because they couldn't get financing because they were colored, and the idea behind that was they wouldn't or couldn't pay their bills.

That had never stopped us from selling to white people who couldn't pay their bills. That's why I repossessed cars or we had someone else do it.

I went out and talked to them, and by day's end, I had their Ford and they had a newer one. I sold them one of the better ones on the lot. On the form I wrote in *W* for "white" in the section that wanted to know their race. They had been able to pay half of it, raw bills the man pulled out of his fat wallet. They had been saving for four years, he said.

I had them come into the office and I filled out the paperwork with them. The woman set silent, as if she thought she ought to, being in the presence of a white man and sitting in an office they might not normally be allowed into.

I hoped Dave wouldn't come back during that process, but I didn't really give a shit, because right then, I didn't give a shit about how things were supposed to be. I had already violated how things were, and in a big way. What I was doing at that moment was nothing.

When I got off that afternoon, I didn't go home. I drove out to see Dash. I knew he wouldn't have the birth certificate ready, but I wanted some company, and the thing was, I didn't really have any friends. Dash wasn't exactly a friend; I don't know what he was, but we could talk and drink beer and I felt good at his place.

When I got out there, I saw his car parked in the yard, and I went straight to the building out back, which was where I figured I'd find him, because, like last time, I could hear the air conditioner out there and none in the house.

I was right. He answered with his usual smile, flashing that gold tooth with the silver star, offered me a beer. I sat on the couch while he sat in his chair facing me.

"You looking rough, my friend."

"Didn't sleep well."

"You look like someone that's done something wrong."

It was just a saying, but he had no idea.

"You know that certificate ain't ready yet. Only work a bit on it a day. Too much of a rush, I'll fuck it up."

"I know. Just thought I'd like a free beer."

He grinned at me. "You know, you're a weird cat, playing all white and stuff, and you're out here with the niggers."

"Just one. You. And I'll just say 'colored.'"

"Try saying 'human.'"

"Oh, now you're going to get all political on me, and I'm the one correcting you."

"No, but you don't make a very good white person, Ed."

"I don't fit anywhere."

"You all right here."

"Thanks."

"I figure you ain't seen any more of Cecil."

"Course not."

"Well, don't think he's forgot. He's kind that will let something stew until it boils over. You might think he's done let it go, but he ain't."

"Guess I'll cross that bridge when I come to it."

"Another beer?"

"Yeah. That would be great."

I don't really remember what else we talked about that day, but when I left it was nearly eight at night. I was parked out in front of Dash's house in my Cadillac and had been for hours, and right then I didn't give a shit. I didn't give a shit about a lot of things.

I drove out into the country, stopped and got the grip out of the trunk and took the bloody rags out of it and threw them into the woods, then I drove down a ways and threw the grip into a creek that had a little wooden bridge over it. The water wasn't deep, but I figured it was highly unlikely anyone would think the grip had anything to do with murder.

I had kept the crowbar. Somebody was doing real detective work, somehow found out I had bought the tarp and crowbar, I could explain a paint-covered tarp being thrown away pretty easy, but why would I throw out a perfectly good crowbar?

When I unlocked my apartment door, the phone was ringing.

It was Nancy.

(36)

I miss you," she said.

"You too. You all right?"

"I think so. I want you in my bed or me in yours."

"You know we can't. Not now. In a month or after you get the money, depending."

"Walter was asking about Frank. He asked where he was. I told him he'd gone fishing."

"Why was he asking?"

"I don't know. I think he likes me. I mean, it's like a little boy liking a girl in grade school. But he wonders about Frank because he thinks if I'm alone, maybe he's going to get lucky."

The way she said that, it sounded very rote. I guessed she was still in shock. Probably we both were. "I don't think I like that," I said.

"You shouldn't. If you're not a little jealous, then what am I worth to you?"

"Tomorrow, you call the police and report him missing. Say he was going to go fishing down at Marvel Creek. There's a lot of Marvel Creeks, so they'll ask where is that, and you say, 'Not the town, the creek. He said it was nearby.' But you don't give them directions. You don't know nothing, but you're worried, because he had been drinking and you told him not to drive, but he got his gear together and went anyway. Took some beers with him. You got all that?"

"Yeah. I got it."

"Then they'll go look, and I bet they find the car right away and probably him too."

"After they find him, you sure I should wait a month to get the insurance?"

"It makes it look like you're so upset, you're not thinking about the money. That you're mourning, and then one day you realize you got to find out about it, and you go in and see your insurance man."

"Yeah. I'm up at the drive-in on Friday nights lot of the time, and my insurance man, Mr. Rose, his daughter and her boyfriend come in. I see them, I always think about that insurance money and how it's waiting there if something should happen to Frank, and now it has."

"He had a car accident. He was drunk and drove off the bridge."

"Right."

"I'd say call the police pretty early tomorrow. You can tell your story about the fishing but say you thought he might not come straight home, fishing or not, 'cause he liked to do the honky-tonks, but now you're worried. It's been too long. That shows why you weren't on this right away. He has some habits, like drinking late, staying out. You weren't really concerned, because that was just his way. We got to create a story, but it needs to be simple and tied to things he really does. That way you can keep up with it."

"I miss you."

"You too. Just follow the script, baby, and we'll be farting nickels through silk pajamas."

(37)

That night I had a few drinks of the hard stuff, to take the edge off, and when I said that to myself, I remembered that's what Mama always said: "I'm having a few just to take the edge off."

I figured if that was true, she had liquored that edge down until it was so dull, you couldn't cut hot butter with it. Still, I took some drinks for just the same reason, and then I went to bed.

I had a hard time sleeping even though I was so exhausted I could hardly stand up. In my head I put the Korean I had killed together with Frank, and sometimes Frank spoke Korean, and in my sort of awake/asleep situation, he would ask me something in Korean, and I kept hitting him with the crowbar saying, "What? What's that? What you want?" Frank was just standing there taking it, and sometimes it was the Korean standing there taking it, wearing Frank's clothes, and the Korean would say in English, "You know this is fucked up, don't you?"

I'd say, "Yes, I know that," and keep hitting him, holding a rifle now, using the stock, sometimes the crowbar.

When I quit thinking about that, I'd think about Dash and the birth certificate and hope that would get done, and then I'd think, Shit, this is all so stupid. I ought to get my sister and mother and go someplace far away. But what place, and how far away, and what about that goddamn insurance money and the drive-in and that fucked-up plot of land with a horse buried on it?

Then I thought about how I hated the idea of those animals just thrown out in the woods, and that was exactly what me and Nancy had done with Frank. We had thrown him out in the water in the woods, and he was a human being.

I had never felt so miserable. The Korean I had been able to justify, that was war, and it was him or me, and Frank might have had it coming, but no matter how much I told myself that, it didn't satisfy me.

I found that I was thinking about how Nancy had spoken with me and how we talked about missing each other, but there was something dry in her voice. I chalked that up to fear. Sure, she missed me, but she missed me because she was scared. I missed her for the same reason. We were the only two people in the world that knew the terrible secret of what we had done.

My stomach did a lot of churning, but at least I didn't throw up my cheeseburger.

(38)

When I got to work the next morning, there was a car parked out front of the office, and when I got out, the driver got out too.

I had never seen him before. He was a thin little man in a too-big but expensive suit, and he had on glasses that made his eyes look like marbles underwater. His hat hung over his face like an awning.

He was carrying a piece of paper. He smiled at me, but it was the kind of smile a frightened kid gives a grown-up he doesn't know.

I walked over to him.

"Are you Ed Edwards?"

"I am."

"I have some bad news and maybe a bit of good news."

"What d'you mean?"

"Dave. He didn't make it."

"Didn't make what?"

"He went in for a checkup, and they found something bad with his heart, sent him right away to the emergency room, and then he got sick when he was there, and it all got worse . . . and, well, he didn't make it."

"Son of a bitch."

"I have this for you."

It was a piece of paper and I read it, but it was like my eyes wouldn't register it. Part of that was the shock of his death, part of it was dealing with the night before. "Just tell me."

"He left you some money, and he sold the car lot."

"Sold it? He just went in the hospital. How could he do all that?"

"It was a deal in motion. The lot over on Margin Street, the owner there, he bought it. They been hammering out the deal for a few weeks."

"Dave was already selling out? He didn't mention it."

"Thought he'd be around longer. It was so quick. Family was taken care of, though. I'm sure he was going to tell you."

I thought maybe not. Dave had been playing the game with me, working it right up until the end. I might have been like a son to him, but if that was so, he damn sure didn't mind steamrolling his son. And then, that could have just been his line of patter, his salesmanship to keep me on to the last minute, maybe in case he got sick. Hell, he knew how bad he was. That son of a bitch.

"He left you a thousand dollars." He handed me the paper. "You can give me the keys to here and take this paper to the bank and they'll pay it out. It's all set up."

I took the paper without really thinking about it and gave the little man the keys. He hadn't even said his name, and frankly, I didn't care what it was. A thousand dollars was all right, it wasn't chicken feed, but I felt blindsided.

I went over to the bank and cashed the check and then I went home and got gloriously drunk and went to bed, and this time I knocked that goddamn edge off good.

I slept deep.

(39)

I didn't go to Dave's funeral. I sent flowers.

About a week went by, and I hadn't even looked for a job. It occurred to me the new owners of the car lot might take me on, seeing as I'd been there for so long and had so much experience and a highly successful sales record.

I figured I'd go see them about a spot on the lot, but with a thousand in the bank along with what I had already stashed, I wasn't in any hurry. I was thinking about the insurance money.

I visited with Mama and Melinda, but I didn't mention I had lost my job at the lot. I'd save that for when I got a new job or got taken on by the new owners at the old one until I could get the drive-in business under mine and Nancy's new management.

I visited with Dash a lot, got Melinda's reimagined birth certificate from him. Other than that, me and him sat around and talked about this and that and drank a lot of beer.

When I wasn't doing that, I sat home waiting for time to go by. I thought about Nancy. I thought about big, stupid Frank and how he'd come close to killing me.

It unnerved me a little.

(40)

Two weeks out from the murder, bright and early one morning, Nancy called.

"I spoke to the police."

"Go on, tell all of it. Don't keep me in suspense."

"They found him."

"Oh."

"Someone saw the car first and then they found him down the creek, not far from the car, called it in. Cop I spoke to, a detective named McGinty, said when they saw Frank's body, it looked as if he had crawled part of the way up the creek before he played out and died."

"Damn. I'll give him this. He was one hell of a beast."

"They asked me the questions I thought they'd ask. But they asked me pretty early if I had an insurance policy on him. I told them I did, of course. They asked to look around the house, and I let them. I didn't want to cause suspicion."

"They're just sniffing. Husband dies, could be the wife set it up somehow. They're right, but that doesn't mean they know for sure. It's part of an investigation. They'll eliminate you. We took care of everything pretty well."

"Should I get a lawyer?"

"Hell no. Don't give them any reason to think anything. You get a lawyer, they start wondering what you need one for, and then things heat up."

"I just wondered."

"No lawyer."

"They said they doubted all that happened to him was a car accident. They think someone got into it with him out there, and maybe Frank was trying to get away, ran off the bridge, and whoever it was went down there and hit him with something."

"I don't think Frank would have tried to get away."

"They said it could be that way, and then McGinty said, 'Could be that someone killed him and put him in the car and tried to make it look like an accident.'"

"He said that?"

"You think I'm just fucking with you? Yeah. He said that."

"All right. Let's say he does think that—that doesn't mean you had anything to do with it. It could be someone he got to dealing with out there, like the detective said. Frank could be a bad drunk. You tell them that?"

"I did."

"Don't give them anything new, don't give them an excuse or a scenario of some kind. They got to work with what they have, and what they got is he's dead and pretty apt to stay that way. They can't pin anything on you or me."

"They don't know about you at all. You're golden."

"I don't like the way you said that."

"It's the truth. I didn't mean anything by it."

"Sorry. I'm just nervous. Listen. Stick with what you know, which isn't much. He went fishing, and he might have gone to the honky-tonks, and that's all you know. He was all right when he left."

"I could say he said he'd been having trouble with someone but say I don't know who."

"No way. That's what I mean. Don't start trying to fix it, because you're trying to fix something that isn't broken. You stick to the simple story. It's easy to remember and it doesn't open any doors for them. You hear?"

"Don't make it an order."

"It's not an order, it's a life-or-death fucking suggestion."

"Okay."

"We're both nervous. A little snappy. But we're all right. We are completely all right. Stay with the story, don't embellish. They know you have an insurance payout, but don't act like you're all that interested in it. Let time go by, like you're grieving and too consumed by it to think about that kind of business."

"I do think about it."

"So do I. But they want to see how much you're thinking about it."

"You're right, of course."

"Good. Stay with it."

"I miss you."

"And I miss you."

"Sure we can't see each other? I really feel lonely."

"You know as well as I do that isn't a good idea."

"I don't like being lonely. That's how I got interested in you, and then it turned to something more. But it started because I was lonely."

I thought there might be a message in that, but I tried to keep her focused. "It's not a great way, but it's the right way. We have to wait."

"One other thing, Ed. Way the body looked, they aren't going to let me cremate it. Not right away. They say the body is evidence. They got it down at the morgue."

"All right. Nothing we can do about that. Just let them think it's murder. As long as they don't think you had anything to do with it, it'll be all right. Besides, it's not what they think. It's what they can prove."

"Okay, Ed. Sure. Kisses," she said, and we hung up.

It wasn't more than two days later when she called again. I always let her call me, not knowing who might be at her home, people wanting their animals buried or some such.

I had been on pins and needles since her last call, but I was glad to hear from her until she said, "They're not going to pay out."

"What do you mean?"

"The insurance people. I know you told me to wait, but what's the difference between two weeks and a month?"

"About two weeks, Nancy. It's two more goddamn weeks."

"I made a decision. Two weeks was long enough, and I played it the right way. I told the guy runs the insurance agency, my agent, Rose, told him I no longer had Frank's checks coming in from the encyclopedias, and I needed to hire someone to help me run the drive-in, the cemetery. I had to start thinking about the money."

"Damn, Nancy."

"Don't be mad."

I was mad, but I knew it was pointless. It was done, and I didn't want to make Nancy think I wasn't on her side. That could ruin things for me and her. Mostly me, I figured. "Tell me what they said."

"I told them I had to check on the policy, and it turns out it wasn't a regular life-insurance policy. It was a death-or-accident policy."

"Well, he's dead, and for all they know, it was an accident."

"They don't quite see it that way."

"How do they see it?"

"The insurance man, Esau Rose—and there's something about that guy. I hate that prick. Who names their kid Esau?"

"I guess his mother. Tell me what he said."

"Rose says that the death part of the insurance means if Frank just keeled over, it would be paid out. You know, natural causes. And the accident part meant just that. Had to be an accident."

"That's what it was. You and I know different, but they don't."

"They might."

"How's that?"

"Told you the cops thought Frank might have been murdered, and Rose thinks so too. And he controls the money. The policy is pretty specific, and he says he doesn't think murder is considered an accident."

"He said that?"

"He did. Went to the cops with it, the cheap bastard. Said it was the cops that were suspicious. But it's him too. The little weasel. I hope his tweed suit itches his ass."

"He smelled a rat?"

"He smelled us. He doesn't know there's an us, but he smelled us anyway. I know he doesn't trust me. He doesn't know about you, but I could see the wheels turning. He's thinking a woman like me, my size, I couldn't have done what was done to Frank. He's thinking I had some man to help me out."

"You don't know any of that."

"Don't snap at me, Ed. It's been a bad morning."

"Sorry. But he doesn't know any of that. You're feeling guilty is all. I'm feeling that way too, but we did it and it's done, and we have to play it cool."

"While we've been playing it cool, the cops came over again. McGinty said Rose said the whole thing didn't smell right. Rose was all smiles with me, saying how he had to check a few things out, but he's telling the cops a different story. He's saying to them he thinks I had something to do with it, not some outsider. I can tell by the questions the cops ask."

"They can't prove anything, and even if Frank was murdered, that's an accident, by God. They'll have to pay."

"If they figure us out, they won't."

"Guess we have to worry about that later. Right now, we don't need to concern ourselves with it. They didn't accuse you."

"Yeah, but the cops are asking how me and Frank got along. I lied, said okay, though we'd had a bit of trouble here and there, but didn't all couples? That kind of stuff."

"Did they buy it?"

"I don't know. This McGinty, he's hard to read. He looks at me like I haven't got any clothes on."

"I can assure you a lot of men look at you that way."

"I'm not doing anything."

"I didn't say that. That's how men are. It's hormones. We aren't worth the powder it would take to blow our asses up. All we want to do is fuck and spend money, and right now, I'm not doing either."

"I like it when you're crude."

"I don't like myself much when I am. What did the cop do?"

"Kept staring at me and asked me the same thing over and over. I kept my story straight. Didn't change it. He said there would be an inquiry."

"All right," I said. "Just play it close to the house. Go to the drive-in, spend more time there than usual. Act normal."

"I don't feel normal."

"Neither do I, honey, and there's a reason for that. This isn't normal, but we got to win the fucking Oscar from here on out."

"I really wanted that money, Ed. It was a plan I thought would work."

"It was a good plan. Frank just wouldn't cooperate. He disagreed with the main feature of our plan. He didn't want to die."

(41)

It wasn't but two nights later when she came over to the apartment. I had told her where I lived a while back, but it was about ten o'clock and I was about to go to bed, and there's a gentle knock at the door.

I answered it, and there she was.

At first, seeing her, I was mad, but then I was glad. I pulled her inside, and we jerked each other's clothes off and ended up in the bedroom. It was a long night and there wasn't much sleeping. The bedsprings squeaked so furiously, I feared the people in the apartment below might complain.

We slept in most of the next day.

When we woke up, even though it was after noon, I went into the kitchen and fixed us some coffee and breakfast while she did her bathroom duties. I had given her a spare toothbrush and a fresh towel.

Breakfast was ready when she came into the kitchen with the towel, using it to dry her hair. She wasn't wearing anything.

"Sit down," I said.

She wrapped the towel around her and sat down, and I put breakfast and a cup of coffee in front of her.

"I know what you're going to say, Ed. That I shouldn't have come here."

"I can't say that. Not after last night."

She smiled, and it really tugged at me. I liked that smile. "It was good, wasn't it?"

"Yeah. Where did you park?"

"Down the block."

"That should be all right. People park all up and down the street here."

"Rose isn't going to authorize the money."

"Can he do that?"

She sipped her coffee. "He can and will. They aren't saying I did anything or had anything done, but it's suspicious enough, he told me, that he couldn't in good conscience pay out the money until there was a full investigation."

"How long can that take?"

"He said it might take a year."

"A year?"

"That's what he said. He knows I had something to do with it, Ed. He's putting off paying me until he thinks the cops can prove I did it. He's a tight-ass company man who does it all by the book. He's a real son of a bitch."

"He's smart is what he is."

"Too smart."

"I don't mean to sound crass, baby, but I was counting on that money."

"You and me both."

I told her about how I had lost my job.

"That's tough. I'm so sorry."

I agreed and poured us more coffee.

"You know what?" she said.

"What?"

"There might be a way to get us together and for it to look all right. You see, they don't know I know you, and you need a job. Right? So I can put you on at the drive-in. I can make you manager. If it should come up, I can say you're doing what Frank used to do, though in truth, Frank didn't do anything but go on the road to sell encyclopedias and drink beer, come home and drink beer, and wipe his dick off on my inner thigh."

"Don't tell me that."

"For a murderer, you're awfully sensitive," she said.

"I guess I am."

"Way we could do is you could go to work for me, and there's a little room there at the drive-in, and the concession has some cooking stuff, so it would be your kitchen. There's a bathroom in that little section, and we can put a bed in there. We can say you needed a job, and since you worked at the car lot, you know how to keep records—"

"That's true. I do."

"We can say you live there and run the place, and I don't like to do that kind of thing anyway. We'll say it's men's business. They love that."

"And all the while, you're giving them the business."

"We both are. What do you think?"

"Not a bad idea. Not at all. That way I'm not just hanging around, and you don't have to sneak over here to see me. And I can quit burning up rent money."

"Housing will be part of your salary, if anyone asks."

I had rent coming up, and I had the thousand dollars in the bank with what I had saved up, and what I'd had before the thousand was good enough when I had a job, but without an income, I would soon be back on a car lot, which I was sick of by that point.

If we weren't going to get that insurance money, maybe

the next best thing would be me managing the drive-in with Nancy.

No reason for the cops to suspect any kind of previous connection between us. For all the cops knew, I was just some guy who'd been looking for a job and I got one there.

(42)

I went to work at the High-Tone Drive-In, and frankly, there wasn't much work to it. I looked at the books and determined the theater had a lot of customers, but tickets were cheap, so that didn't bring in a lot of cash. The real money came from the concession, all the teenagers coming in and eating like piranhas with a blooded cow in the water, but even that didn't make as much money as I'd thought. The real money wasn't all that real. I got my cut, it wasn't as good as the car lot.

As for the cemetery, activity was slow. Most folks just got a shovel, buried Fido in the backyard.

I thought about how more money could be made. During the week, Nancy mostly worked the pimple-faced girl, but now and again she had extra help on the weekends, which was when you had all the teenagers. The help was paid cheap and they worked like it.

I thought maybe if we paid the workers more and had more of them, they might be happier and give customers better service, and that might help improve business. Nancy wasn't biting.

I thought we could let Walter go. I could take tickets, or Nancy could. That would save some dough. But she wouldn't hear of it. He did all the repairs at the place, and she said we could get him to learn how to actually taxidermy the dogs and cats when needed, and we could bump up prices on everything from burying critters to popcorn, and we could work more instead of hiring more teenagers at a higher price.

I was beginning to think the businesses weren't doing well due not only to Frank, but to Nancy herself.

Worst part was me and Walter didn't like each other. It had been hate at first sight, and in time it became worse. I hardly spoke to him. I didn't want to hear his voice. I hated turning my back on him. It made me nervous.

Now and again I saw him going up to the house to get something or other. I'd be at the drive-in doing this and that, and I couldn't get my mind off him going up there, and I'd end up going up there myself.

I found him sitting at the kitchen table a few times, having a cup of coffee with Nancy. I didn't like that at all. Nancy said a man could have a cup of coffee without it being romantic, but I still didn't like it.

I thought about how me and her had gotten together, and that hadn't taken much, and Walter, he was a big, handsome fellow, and, well, I didn't like it. In a nutshell, I was jealous.

The jealousy worked two ways. I found that out one night due to the daughter of the insurance man, Esau Rose. The girl came regularly to the drive-in with her boyfriend, and they would come up to the concession stand together. She was about seventeen, I figured, long-legged and tan with tumbling blond hair. Where Nancy looked like sweaty sheets and the clinging aroma of musk, this girl, she looked like sweetness and clouds and long romance. She always wore simple but well-fitting clothes and gold earrings dangling against her tanned skin.

The boy she came with was a football type, handsome and broad-shouldered, and the way he moved, conducted himself, you couldn't help but get the feeling he was as dense as the Amazon rain forest.

I had seen them both before at the drive-in, so it wasn't the first time I had noticed her. But this night I'm talking about, I was working the concession with the pimple-faced girl and Nancy, as the other help had decided they were done with the job. I marked that up to Nancy being a tightwad.

When the girl came in, it was like a warm light came in with her. Now, I know how that sounds, sexual and all, but it wasn't like that. It was like finding a puppy beside the road. If you had any kind of heart, you wanted to bring it home and feed it and take care of it.

Well, I know how that sounds too, but I assure you, it wasn't like that.

The boy swaggered up with his wallet in his hand, his mouth hanging open, his eyes not quite making contact with mine. He looked at the candy under the glass, pursed his lips, and studied the popcorn popping in the machine like there might be a variety of choices there. "Give me a hot dog and a Coke, one of the big ones, and we want the big bag of popcorn. Two boxes of those chocolate-covered almonds too."

The girl, all smiles, said, "Reggie, I'll have a hot dog as well."

"Sure," Reggie said.

Something about Reggie made me want to push his face in.

The girl looked at me. Her eyes were so innocent, I hated that she had to live in this world, hated that one day she would find the world a lot less innocent than she felt it was now.

"You're new," she said, turning her head in a way that made me think even more of a puppy.

"Just went to work here recently."

148

Nancy looked over at me, then at the girl on the other side of the concession, and Nancy's black eyes looked like crude oil boiling.

The pimple-faced girl was helping another couple, so me and Nancy put together the girl and her boyfriend's order.

"You got only one drink," I said. "Do you want another?"

The girl looked at me like I was the only person in the universe. "Make it a small Dr Pepper."

Nancy, who was now close beside me, said, "I'll get that."

"You have such lovely skin," the girl said to Nancy.

"Thanks," Nancy said. It was like she had to say it around teeth that were biting the head off a kitten.

They gathered up their food, and the boy said, "Come on, Julie. Let's get back. I think the killing is about to happen."

When they went out, I wondered how Julie had ended up with that idiot, and then I thought I might be Nancy's idiot.

*　　　*　　　*

When Walter finally went home at night—he had a habit of hanging around for long stretches—Nancy would have me come up to the house, or she'd come to my place in the concession building to visit with me. That was damn nice, but I sure wasn't getting any richer.

Something about that girl, Julie Rose, the insurance man's daughter, was kind of like a soothing salve on my soul, and I started looking forward to seeing her Friday nights, or sometimes it was Saturday. She and her boyfriend nearly always came. We spoke more as time went by, me and her. Nothing serious, just the usual across-the-counter small talk you made with someone you didn't really know. I liked seeing her, though, and I really started pushing to be behind the concession on Friday nights.

In time I didn't want to go up to the house and see Nancy,

preferred she came to see me, because I went up there, came to the back door where I finished Frank off, it got so I expected to see him out there with that stick, his face all knotted, his eyes almost shut, smiling at me, showing me his missing teeth, his bloody mouth.

(43)

One night after the drive-in had closed down and Walter had left to go wherever he stayed, some burrow, I figured, Nancy came to the drive-in, and we went into my little room and did the nasty for an hour or two.

She had brought a bottle of the good stuff, and she got up without putting anything on, turned on the light, got the bottle and a couple of fruit jars out of my little nest of assorted dishes, and poured a generous amount of that liquid heat in the jars. She took her time bringing them over to the bed because she wanted to have me see what it was I'd been having and could have again.

She stood tall and her breasts were poked out, and pretty soon the sheet over me was poked out too. She sat down on the bed with her back against the wall and gave me my drink.

I had been lying down, but now I sat up and put my back against the wall the same as her. We were so close, I could feel heat coming off her. It was like sitting next to a forest fire. I sipped from the jar. It made me tingle all over.

"I been thinking. I know a way we can get that money, Ed."

"What do you mean?"

"I figure any day now, I'll get word they aren't paying out, because they released Frank's body to his mother, not me."

"They did?"

"Just said it. Yeah."

"Hell, Nancy. I thought you had already given up on that money. I know I have."

"From the insurance company, yeah. But we can get as much from Esau Rose as we would have from the insurance."

Some scenarios tried to form in my mind about how we might get that much money without the insurance paying it, but I came up with nothing. I didn't say anything. I sipped my drink. I knew Nancy liked to be a little dramatic, so I waited.

"That girl. Julie."

"The daughter of the insurance guy, Esau Rose."

"Yeah. The pretty one you like talking to so much at the concession."

"Don't be silly. She's a customer."

"She's a cute little trick of a customer with a tight sweater and a fat ass."

I should have let that go, but I didn't. "I wouldn't say it was fat."

"See? I was right. You are looking at her."

"Hey, I'm not dead. But she's just a kid."

"A ripe kid. But listen here, Ed. Get your mind off her ass and think about what I'm saying. This is where I see some irony coming in, this plan I got. What we do is we take her, and we demand money for her father to get her back. The money owed on the insurance. Not the exact amount, that might be too much, and it might get figured out if it's the same. They might look to me, since they're already suspicious about Frank's death. But we ask for an amount in that ballpark. Old man Rose has money. He's got it from cheating everyone on their insurance. Not wanting to pay out claims."

"Insurance money doesn't come out of his pocket, darling. And I'm not liking this idea much at all."

"Will you at least hear me out?"

I decided I would, and then I'd tell her we wouldn't do that because it was stupid.

"What we do is, we watch her a bit. Know she comes here on Fridays or Saturdays. Nearly every Friday, and when she leaves, if you're set, you could follow her and maybe catch her when the boy lets her off. You'd have to deal with him."

"Deal with him?"

"I'm not saying you hurt him bad, but you could discourage him from giving you any trouble. You go prepared. Knock him down or out. Grab the girl, and we can put her up somewhere. We need to find a place, figure that out, but we stash her and set the ransom. Rose pays us off, we return the girl."

I thought about that for a moment. It was something I was all set to dismiss, but then I got to thinking we could ask for fifty thousand dollars, which was more than the insurance payout. We could ask for that, and that much money, we got that, we were set. We could get married, and that way I would have access to the property Nancy had. She had at least inherited that after Frank's death. We could sell the drive-in and the cemetery off, those not being the moneymaking businesses I'd thought, and we could use that money to buy a car lot. I understood that business. I would be a lot better at it than Dave, and he was good. I played it right, I could own a string of them, have other people doing the job I used to do, and I could manage things. I'd be sitting pretty. And so would Nancy, of course.

I began to think about being a big shot all over again. "We would have to really plan ahead," I said.

She smiled at me. She knew her fish. She had dangled the bait of quick money, and I bit.

(44)

When Julie and her boyfriend came to the drive-in, I would study their pattern. They always came for the first feature, but usually after that, they left.

That made it about nine p.m. Mostly Friday nights, sometimes Saturdays.

One night about eight thirty, I went over to the barn, garage, whatever you want to call it, pulled Nancy's car around out back of the house, and waited. I sat on the back porch and drank coffee and watched the drive-in to see when Julie and Alley Oop left. There was plenty of light from that big sign, so when they came out the exit, I would be able to see them go.

I sat and looked at that big bright sign, those lights that seemed like a big golden finger pointing skyward. Place hadn't lived up to my expectations, and though I'm not a superstitious man, and not religious, I liked to believe, same as the first time I saw those lights, that the golden finger was pointing up toward my success. It was just a little game I played, and it occurred to me if we got that money, maybe we wouldn't sell the place. We could get someone to run it, hopefully not Walter. Because if I talked Nancy into keeping the place, that's what she'd want, her cousin to run it. I didn't like that, but then I decided I could live with that if I had to.

I got to thinking we could buy a nice place over in the Bright Grove division, which was just as far from a trailer house or dingy apartment as you could imagine. It was miles and thoughts away from the kind of place where my father grew up.

I imagined we could have a pool. Thought about how Nancy would look in some skimpy bikini, her skin dark and the sun bright, both of us sitting in those big stretch lawn chairs with tall, cool drinks in our hands, those little umbrella rigs stuck down in them next to an olive or a round pickled onion. I had never had a drink like that, but I had seen them in movies, and I thought that was what I wanted to have, at least once.

And a house with two or three stories, a bedroom on top where I could look out the window and see the pool, a tall fence surrounding the backyard. And from there I could also see beyond the pool and the fence, see way on out.

We'd have a lawn and someone to tend to it, keep the flowers growing in big long flower beds. We could design the flowers to look special, not just in rows. Maybe we could get enough land to have a big garage where we could park the Cadillac, maybe a newer model, and some other car. A sports car.

Course, I'd have to make money from those car lots I planned to own as well, but if I played my cards right, I could do that. I could . . .

That's when I saw Julie's boyfriend's car pull out of the drive-in. I sat the cup on the steps and slipped into Nancy's car, and when I saw which way they turned, I drove around the house and on out to the highway.

At first, I thought I'd lost them, as the kid was driving kind of fast, but then as I went along, I saw taillights that looked like the taillights to his car. I didn't get right on their ass but close enough to be certain it was them.

They didn't go on into town, where Julie lived. I'd looked that up in the phone book, got the address, and drove over there to check things out. She lived in the kind of place I'd been thinking about before, and I realized that's why I was thinking about it.

The Rose residence had a big brick wall around it, and there were lights on the wall. Tall oaks and hickory trees were rising up above the fence, and there were some other kinds of trees you could see through the barred gate lining the drive. It was a house made of white stone with a dark roof, three stories, like I had been imagining.

But that's not where they went.

They turned on the road Nancy and I had taken when we brought Frank's body to the bridge. They even turned where the bridge was. I pulled over and switched off my headlights and watched their taillights go along.

It was a bright night, and I could see well enough to drive without lights if I went slow, and I did. I crossed that rickety bridge. The railing was still broken where we had pushed Frank and his car over.

The idea of that bridge, and him down there, and what we had done to him came back to me in a bloodred rush. I felt as if I were crossing the bridge under which the troll in the Three Billy Goats Gruff story lived.

No troll came out to bother me as I rattled over the bridge, but I'll tell you, a stained conscience did. That got me thinking about this plan of ours, and I got sort of sick to my stomach. But then I thought about the fact that we weren't going to hurt anyone. We were going to hold her for ransom. I might have to hit the kid with a sap or something, but beyond that, it was just kidnap Julie and take the money and give her back.

I'd have to wear a mask, of course. I'd have to do that so I wouldn't be recognized. Maybe I could disguise my voice. It was stuff to think about. But tonight, this was just reconnaissance.

I finally saw taillights turning at the end of a long narrow trail that led into the woods. I stopped the car and leaned over so I could see out the passenger window. The car's taillights went out at the far end. I knew what that meant.

Julie and her boyfriend were about to engage in a timeless human tradition. The thought of her lying under that big idiot made my skin crawl. I couldn't wait to hit him with the blackjack.

(45)

Next morning, me and Nancy drove out to where the couple had parked. The little road ended there, and there was a big place where you could turn around, a spot near where the creek ran wide and deep, almost like a river.

We walked around, checking the location out. A lot of people had come there over the years to fish or park and have sex. There were a number of tied-off rubbers lying on the ground.

Nancy kicked one of the rubbers, said, "There's someone's family that isn't happening. Julie's, maybe."

I knew she was trying to get under my skin, because she didn't like that I had noticed Julie, and she knew too that it was more than just looking at an attractive girl. It was looking into my past and wishing I had met someone like her when I was a kid. Back then, the idea of being with some white girl bothered me, because I knew I had the blood in me, and if a girl found out, if anyone found out, I'd be like a man floating in space. Lost and lonely in the cold emptiness. And maybe swinging from a tree somewhere.

We got back in the car and sat there a moment.

"You think they always come here?" Nancy said.

"Probably. I need to follow them a bit more, see what they do.

If they make this a habit, one night, I'll knock him on the noggin. I'll need you to grab her while I'm dealing with him. We'll need masks, disguises of some sort."

"That sounds right."

"And we'll need someplace to keep her where she can't get away."

"I've been thinking about that. I got some ideas."

"Want to share?"

"Not yet. I'm still considering."

We drove home and took off our clothes without even thinking about it. We could feel what the other needed. While we were making love, I closed my eyes, and with each thrust of my hips, I'm ashamed to say, I was thinking of Julie.

(46)

After we made love, still lying in bed, Nancy said, "I got it figured now. We got to do it in a way she won't know where she is, of course, and we got to do it in a way we don't always have to watch after her, but we'll know she's taken care of, can't escape, won't get hurt."

"Obviously."

"We rent a backhoe, dig a big hole out in the cemetery like we're going to plant another horse or such, and then we build a nice box in there with an air pipe. We fix it so the box is barely covered with dirt, and we put an air pipe up out of it, and we can take her out and put her in the garage part of the time, but at night she goes in there. That way we don't have to watch her every minute."

"I don't know. Sounds kind of precarious."

"She'd just be there at night, and there would be the air pipe, and we could put her inside late and take her out early. She wouldn't be there all the time."

"We'd need really good disguises, taking her in and out like that."

"We could leave her in there most of the time, then, just take her out for bathroom trips, feed her something."

"No. I like that idea a lot less. The first way is best."

"Halloween mask might do it."

"It's not Halloween, so I don't think that's something you're going to buy anywhere."

"I got some masks at the drive-in. One of the features we had during Halloween came with a bunch of free masks we were supposed to hand out. We handed out a few, but in the end, we just left them in the box. It was more trouble than it was worth. Handing them out didn't make the picture any better. It wasn't that good a gimmick. We gave out Halloween candy instead."

"I got a change to your idea. How about this? We rent a little skip loader, and we dig that hole in the floor of the smaller building out back. It's dirt, so that wouldn't be any trouble. We put the box in there and keep a blindfold over her eyes. When we finish, we give her back, we can fill up the hole, maybe put some concrete in pretty fast. I know how to do that, how to build the forms to pour the concrete."

"That's too much, Ed. We take her out of that hole, she'll never know where she was. We just fill it back in, and we don't rent the backhoe or skip loader. That's just another connection. We shovel it out, and when it's over, we fill it back in."

"That's a lot harder than you might think."

"I know how hard it is. Why do you think we threw those dead dogs in the woods? But this, we're talking about a lot of money, Ed. A lot of money. I can sweat a little, I need to. Can you?"

I said that I could, and from that point on, we had a plan.

(47)

Those masks were ugly things. There were three kinds. A devil mask, which was red with horns sticking up. A mask that looked like you had a bat on your face. And the third kind, a regular Lone Ranger mask. They were cheap plastic, but that devil mask and that bat mask, those were pretty damn unnerving when you put them on. The Lone Ranger mask, well, I had an idea for that.

I studied myself in the mirror wearing the devil mask. My hair could be seen, so I decided I'd wear a hat or some such. I'd have to dress in clothes I didn't normally wear.

Some of Frank's clothing was still in the closet, and though all of it was too big for me, the pants too long, I decided I could make something out of that. Seemed appropriate, to wear a dead man's clothes.

I followed Julie and her boyfriend a few more weekend nights, and they always went to that place. I thought the way to do it would be for us to park down there early. Park the car away from the spot where they went, but nearby, and I could hide down there in the woods and wait. When the car started rocking, I'd come out and duck along, drag that cretin boyfriend out, and hit him with the blackjack enough to adjust his way of thinking. Certainly enough to wipe that smirk off his face.

Nancy could grab the girl, put a pillowcase over her head, tie her hands behind her back, and we'd tote her off to the car, take her to the prepared hiding place.

Things like that sound easy when you talk about it.

I dug a hole in the storage building, where we kept the little dog coffins and the crosses and such for the animals.

I got the hole done, I used one of the big crates they had in there in case another horse or a donkey died, and fitted it into the ground. I cut a hole in the lid and bought some drainpipe and rigged it so it went down into the box, just into the hole. I sealed up around the hole with plumbing putty.

The box was so big, the top of it was almost out of the hole. That way it was easy to get into. I put a sheet of plywood over that, and then I sprinkled dirt on the top of it, the pipe just sticking out.

To make sure it was all right, I got down in the box and had Nancy put the lid on. It was creepy down there, dark as the spaces between the stars. I could breathe all right, though, and dark as it was, it being day, some light came down the pipe and made a golden circle on my chest. I thought about a Poe story I read, about a man who had been buried alive.

It was creepy business.

I called up for Nancy to take the lid off. It wasn't on there so good right then that I couldn't have gotten out, but I wanted to have some idea how that lid worked. I was going to put clamps all along the side of the box so I could lock the lid down, but I hadn't done that yet.

"Nancy, lift the lid."

I lay there awhile with that golden beam on my chest, and then there was a shadow over the beam; Nancy leaning over to look down the pipe, I figured.

"Come on, let me out of here."

A moment later the pipe was pulled out and the lid was lifted. I crawled out, sat on the edge of the hole.

"You took your time."

"I didn't want to damage the pipe."

"I'm going to fasten it in there better, so you lift up on the pipe, it lifts the lid. After the clamps have been loosened, of course. I have to add those."

"What was it like down there?"

"Dark. I don't know, Nancy. That seems awfully cruel. Down there just that short time, I was pretty claustrophobic."

"It's a lot of money, Ed."

"So it is. I'm going to go to the hardware store, get some clamps."

(48)

Before long, we had things set.

It was Wednesday when we had it all done. We were just waiting on Friday. I helped clean up at the drive-in. At the back of it, a tree had dropped a limb on the tin-sheet fence, tore it up bad. I had to get Walter to go out back and help me tear down the ruined sheet and put up another one. It wasn't hard work, but moving that tin could be dangerous if you did it alone because it was wobbly and the edges were sharp.

Walter helped me move the limb. I put it aside to be thrown away later. We started undoing the bolts in the tin so we could replace it with another sheet. I had the new sheet delivered right next to the fence, so it wasn't much of a job.

We moved the old sheet out and put up the other one, and Walter held it in place while I drilled new connections into it and fastened it to the metal frame that ran along the fence.

Being with Walter made me nervous. There was just something about the guy. I figured once me and Nancy were married, I got my hands on the land, and we had that money, I was going to send Walter packing with a bag of popcorn and five dollars in severance. I can't explain it, but I loathed that guy.

"You and Nancy spend a lot of time together," he said.

"Yeah. We work together, Walter. Just like you and her."

"You seem to spend a lot of time together that isn't work time."

"Are you snooping on us?"

"Watching out for her."

"I think she's old enough to watch out for herself. She can drive a car and everything. Look, Walter. Let it go. Me and her, we get along."

"Her husband hasn't been dead that long."

"Guess he's been dead long enough. How long does he have to be dead? Is there, like, some kind of set time limit? Does he get less dead or more dead as time goes on?"

"You have a smart mouth, Edwards. I don't much like it."

"You don't have to like it. It's not meant to be liked."

"I think you might be taking advantage of Nancy. You know what I'm thinking?"

He said this as I was screwing one of the bolts down. "No. What are you thinking, and how much does it hurt you to do it?"

"There's that smart mouth again. What I'm thinking is you're a fellow moving in on a dead man's wife. While she's soft about things, hurt from the loss."

"Is she that bad hurt?"

"It was her husband."

"Husbands come in all stripes. Frank, she says he was a bastard. That he hurt her."

"I think you might lead her down the wrong path."

"What are you getting at?"

"I'm saying I think you're a heel."

"Yeah. Hold that fucking tin straight."

He adjusted, did a good job from there on out.

When I was putting up the tools, I said, "Listen, Walter. You're here because Nancy likes you. You're a cousin. But me and her, we got our own thing going, and I want you to keep your nose out of it."

"You came around before Frank was dead, bub."

"So?"

"So, then he gets dead, and then you move into the drive-in, and you're up to the house a lot, and I don't think it's just for a cup of coffee, a slice of cake."

"Oh, I get a nice slice of cake now and again."

"What's that supposed to mean?"

"Just what you think it means. I'm not trying to make out like we're not together. We met over a used car. That's it. We kind of hit it off. Frank had that wreck, died, and then we got cozy. Just worked out that way."

"Did it? It was just like that, huh?"

"You know what I'm thinking, Walter? I'm thinking you're thinking you might like to be Nancy's kissing cousin."

"Shut your mouth."

I had hold of a hammer from the toolbox. I pulled it out and held it when I spoke to him.

"You can settle down and accept things like they are or you can hit the road. It's not like you're all that good at much. Mostly you just show up and take tickets, pick up a check, hang your tongue out when you see Nancy, probably jack off in the bathroom thinking about her, then glare at me and go home. I could take tickets."

"Nancy is okay with me working here."

I let the hammer hang loose at my side.

"That's all that keeps you here, her being okay with you. And that could change. You know, I might have more clout with Nancy than you think. I might get up one morning, roll out from between her legs, my dick still wet, and say something to her that makes you hit the road with a rip in your pants."

Walter looked at me hard enough to tickle my backbone, and

then he started walking across the lot. I watched as he got to the concession stand. His car was parked in front of it. He got in and drove off.

I hoped I had pissed him off enough to make him decide to move on, maybe get a job pumping gas and changing oil.

Still, there was something about that whole encounter that didn't sit right with me. It was like he was acting out a scene.

I decided I was growing paranoid. All kinds of things didn't seem right anymore. The one that seemed the least right was the fact that I was becoming accustomed to being a murderer.

Walter didn't get that job pumping gas and changing oil. Next night, he was back at the ticket booth, sullen as ever. I tried to steer clear of him as much as possible. I didn't like what he might bring out in me, what monster might surface.

(49)

Thursday night I spoke to Nancy with Walter in hearing distance, with the pimple-faced concession-stand girl in hearing distance as well, and said how I had to leave town because my grandmother was sick.

"You got to go, go," Nancy said. "I know she's sick, you got to be there, but I need you to be back here soon as you can."

"Sure. It's nothing deadly. But she's awful sick. She asked for me."

All of this was a lie, of course. The idea was to explain why I wasn't around. I was going to be spending a lot of my time watching out for Julie down in that box and sometimes in a chair near the box. We had worked out how we would take her up to the house to go to the bathroom. We were going to put the Lone Ranger–style mask on her, but we were stapling black wool to the inside of the mask. The straps on the mask would hold it on, and the thick wool behind the eyeholes would keep Julie from seeing out.

I had to be careful for the week we figured it would take to get our plan done, make sure Walter, or for that matter anyone other than Nancy, didn't see me around the house.

Night I left with the grandma excuse, I drove back later and parked the car in the garage, closed it up and went up to the house and sat in the dark and had a pimento cheese sandwich and a Coke.

Nancy stayed at the drive-in puttering about until all the cars were gone and Walter and the concession girl were gone too. I thought she stayed up there with him a little long, but then again, it seemed she should. She had to play things right and not look in too big a hurry to go to a supposedly empty house. I had to be gone a day before she did the sick act or it was too much going on in the same day and could look connected immediately.

The idea was, tomorrow night she'd tell Walter she didn't feel so good, that she was having her time of the month and might even have a cold on top of it. If she was better, she'd be back the next night, but if not, would Walter run things, since I'd be out of town for a few days? I figured he'd jump at that, a chance to show how well he could do what I did, which, when you got right down to it, was handle soda and popcorn. It was enough to make him feel like a swinging dick for a while.

Then me and her would drive out to Julie and the dumbass's spot. We'd park the car away from it and wait out in the woods with our masks, and when the time was right, we'd get it done.

*   *   *

The night Walter was working in my place, about an hour before Julie and her boyfriend left the drive-in, me and Nancy drove out there. I had scoped out a spot just down from there where I could park Nancy's car up in the brush and it couldn't be seen from the road. I liked it because there was a narrow trail that led out of there and into the woods near where Julie and the cretin would be parked.

We got our gloves and masks, and I got my hat to cover my hair, and Nancy, she had a silly blue Easter hat with a feather in it, and she put that on. We looked ridiculous. I had on some of Frank's old clothes, and I had the pants cuffed and the sleeves on the shirt rolled up to my elbows. That shirt and pants were so big on me, I could damn near jump in a circle inside of them. I wore a pair of my own shoes, but I decided I'd get rid of them with the clothes in case they left a footprint. I had read where someone left a footprint and the cops matched it to the prints on the guy's shoes or some such, so I was going to avoid that possibility. I picked up the rope ties for both of them, the mask for Julie, and a flashlight, which I didn't turn on, and we made our way to the drop spot.

Out in the woods, we sat on the ground and looked through where the brush was thin, and we could see the spot where they would be parked.

In a short time, we got hot and sticky and took off our masks and hats and placed them on the ground and waited. Mosquitoes kept buzzing around our ears, and they bit right through our clothes. Bit? Is that what mosquitoes do, bite? Or do they poke you and suck the blood out, like a syringe? Hell, I don't know. I sat there and thought about stuff like that, and we whispered a little but not about much.

Minutes ticked by as if wearing concrete boots.

Finally, there were car lights.

We put on our hats and masks.

It was the wrong car.

(50)

"That's not them," Nancy said. "That's the wrong car."

"When you're right, you're right."

"What now?"

I thought on it for a moment. "Let's wait awhile, see if this car leaves before they get here."

"Unlikely. They park next to each other, then the game's off," Nancy said.

"Give it some time."

The car started rocking. It didn't last but three or four minutes and then it quit rocking. It wasn't exactly true romance.

The driver rolled the window down and tossed out what I figured was a used rubber. I could see the woman struggling with something inside the car, and I figured she was pulling her panties up. In a moment she stopped. The man turned on the headlights and backed the car out, and away they went.

They hadn't been gone but a minute or two, about the same time it took for lover boy to squirt his seed, before there were more headlights.

We waited, hoping.

It was them.

They parked and the headlights went out. I got up, but Nancy caught my hand.

"No. Let's let them get started. That's the way to surprise them."

I squatted down beside her. I knew what she was doing. She wanted to make sure I knew Julie was being fucked, and she wasn't going to let me take her before the fucking started.

It was a lesson she was teaching me.

I crouched there and watched the car rock, and I admit, the whole thing bothered me, and I wasn't sure why it bothered me. She was underage was part of it, and I couldn't decide if I felt brotherly toward her or if it was something else, like that night I'd dreamed of her while making love to Nancy. I figured it was best not to think about it.

After a bit, Nancy tugged at my shirt to let me know she thought it was time. I put on my devil mask and hat, and Nancy did the same, and without turning on the flashlight, we went out there.

I walked fast, and when I came to the window, I struck it with the blackjack and cracked the glass. I hit it again, and this time lover boy opened the door, trying to hit me with it. I moved away from it, and as he stepped out, I sapped him right behind his left ear.

He did a funny little hop backward and hit the open door, caus-ing it to shut. The car was holding him up, but for good measure I sapped him again on the same side of the head. When he went down, I hit him once more, just to be sure.

I wanted to be sure again, but Nancy said, "Devil. Get it together."

By that time, Julie had tried to open the door and jump out of the car, but Nancy grabbed her. Nancy was strong.

I rolled lover boy on his stomach and tied his hands behind his back and gave him a swift kick in the ribs. He grunted.

I went around the car and saw that Nancy had Julie on the

ground, facedown, and she was tying her hands behind her back. When she had that done, she said, "Get up, bitch."

Julie was crying as she stood up, Nancy hanging on to the rope she had used to tie Julie's hands. I pulled the mask we had fixed up for her, the one with the black wool on it, out of my shirt pocket, snapped the elastic band around her head, and settled the mask over her face.

When that was done, I used the flashlight so we could guide Julie through the brush, onto the trail, and to our car.

When we got her there, I started to put her in the back seat, but Nancy said, "Uh-uh."

She had me open the trunk, and we lifted her in there, used some more rope to tie her feet.

I closed the trunk, turned off the flashlight, and drove us out.

(51)

I untied Julie's feet and hands and helped her into the box, all the while her saying, "Why are you doing this to me?"

"We just want money," Nancy said.

We were both using rough voices, hoping we wouldn't be recognized. We made a point of it because Julie had spoken with both of us at the concession a few times.

"Money?" Julie said and turned her head to look around, even though with that mask on, she couldn't see any more than she would have at the bottom of a coal mine. It was rigged so she couldn't even look down and under it.

"Your daddy's going to pay us some money, dear."

I told her she had to step down into the box, and she hesitated for only a moment and then did just that.

"Lie down," I said. "It's a box, but there's plenty of room."

She started sniffing. I had her lie on her back.

She said, "Please don't rape me."

"No one's going to rape you," I said.

I had screwed some metal loops into the inner sides of the box, and I put the rope around Julie's hands again, one on each hand this time, and I tied the other ends to the loops inside. Then I tied her feet together, but loosely, and ran that rope through another loop at the foot end of the box.

"We're going to put a lid on this box," I said.

"No. No. Please, God, no."

"And I'll fasten it shut with clamps. No use in struggling, you'll just make the ropes tighter than they need to be."

"Why don't you give her a massage, Devil?"

"I just want her to know she's safe."

"Safe?" Nancy said.

I turned my attention back to Julie. "I'm going to put the lid on and fasten the clamps. I'll come back later and check on you."

"Or I will," Nancy said.

"We'll bring you water then, some food. You shouldn't be here long, and we will take you out in the morning."

"The morning? Oh Jesus, don't leave me in this box."

"We'll take you out and let you go to the bathroom and take care of you out of the box, but you'll have to go back inside now and then."

"Give us any trouble," Nancy said, "and you'll stay in that god-damn box shitting and pissing on yourself, you hear me?"

"Yes, ma'am," Julie said.

The way she said that, all schoolgirl polite, I almost pulled her out of there and drove her home, but instead I gritted my teeth and, with Nancy's help, put the lid on and fastened it down.

Me and Nancy took off our masks and hats. I slipped the plywood over the box, then we fastened the air pipe through the hole in the plywood and the top of the box, took shovels, and put a thin layer of dirt over the plywood. With that pipe sticking up, I don't know why we bothered with the dirt, but at that moment it seemed the right thing to do. Way Nancy saw it, things went sideways, we could pull the pipe and throw more dirt into the hole and no one would know she was there. That, of course, meant the worst for Julie, but it was an idea Nancy had, and she liked to elaborate on it from time to time.

When we finished, I could barely hear Julie crying down there.

(52)

We went up to the house, me pushing a wheelbarrow with a shovel laid in it. We hid the masks and hats and gloves in the attic. I took off Frank's clothes and changed into mine, went out and stuck the clothes and shoes in a big black barrel out back used for burning trash. I got some kerosene that was used for fueling cookouts and squirted that into the barrel. I squirted until the plastic bottle was empty. Nancy had also changed, and she put her clothes in there too, just in case Julie might later remember what we had been wearing. I set the stuff on fire, and we sat on the back porch while it burned.

It took a while, but all of it burned. I sprayed the sides of the barrel with the water hose when the fire went out. I tipped the barrel and raked out the stuff that was left, buttons and so on. I raked it all out and shoveled it into the wheelbarrow and let it cool in the night air. Tomorrow, I would bag it and make sure it was put out for the garbage truck.

We went to bed. I slept miserable, lying there in a dead man's bed. Every time I dropped off, I thought I could hear Julie crying and whimpering. It sounded like it was coming from under the bed.

I woke up and was almost tempted to look under the bed to be certain, that's how strong the dream was.

Nancy was fast asleep.

In the kitchen I filled a glass with water and sat in the dark at the table. I looked out the window and I could see the drive-in sign. The light was out, but it was outlined in the moonlight. It seemed alien, like a rocket ship from Mars that had landed quietly.

I sipped my water, went into the bedroom quietly, and got dressed. While I was doing that, Nancy woke up.

"What are you doing?"

"I can't sleep."

"She's all right."

"I know. I'm just nervous. We need to mail the note."

Nancy sat up. "Turn on the light."

I turned on the light.

"We don't need to mail it during the night, Ed."

"I know. Just thought we should get it ready. Then I can drive it into town and put it in a mailbox."

"Don't be silly. Someone sees you dropping off a letter in the middle of the night, remembers that, you'll have put our asses in a crack."

"Guess you're right. I'm just anxious."

"You're always slowing me down. Now I'm slowing you down. That boyfriend of hers has probably worked his way out of his hand ties by now, driven home, and told everyone what happened. The cops are already out searching. In the morning we'll put together the note. I can take it into town and drop it off, go by the store and pick up some groceries. Make it all seem like a casual town run. No one is going to think I'm mailing a ransom note. You're supposed to be visiting your grandmother, remember."

"About that. Say the cops do get onto us or they're curious, they ask where I was during that time, what do I say? I don't have a grandmother I can visit."

"I hadn't thought of that."

"Neither had I. That's a hole in the plan."

Nancy sat quietly with her knees drawn up, her elbows resting on them, her head in her hands.

"Say you actually just wanted to get away but was afraid you said that, I might fire you. You went driving up-country, slept in your car, and just cleared your head."

"I can't prove any of that."

"They can't disprove it. It's one of those things someone might do who has lost their job and is now working at a shitty drive-in."

"All right. It's more likely no one will ask."

"Exactly. You're being a nervous Nellie."

I finally turned off the light and went back to bed.

In the morning, we wrote the ransom note, said in the note we'd call the next morning and to be by the phone. We wrote that if Esau Rose wanted to see his daughter alive again, he needed fifty thousand dollars, and we'd let him know how to make the exchange. We told him we knew the cops knew Julie was missing, but it was best he not bring them with him. That wouldn't be good for Julie.

After we wrote the note, Nancy put it in an envelope, then went out and got the newspaper that had been tossed in the yard, brought it in, and spread it out on the kitchen table.

There was no mention of the kidnapping.

"That's because they're keeping it quiet," I said. "They're not wanting to alert everyone. They're waiting to hear from us. They probably have lover boy put away somewhere so he won't blab. That's good. It means the police are taking it serious, and so is Rose."

Nancy got dressed and took the letter to town.

I got my mask, hat, and gloves and went out to the shed with a paper bag that Nancy had packed with food. I put the mask and hat on, the gloves, raked the dirt off the plyboard, lifted the pipe out of it, unlatched the lid.

Julie was trembling, covered in sweat. It looked like she had just washed her hair.

I spoke to her, untied her, and helped her out of the box. She was weak and seemed to have forgotten how to walk. Her legs were like rubber. "My legs and arms are numb."

I helped her to a chair we had there for her, and she sat. "Kind of flex your arms and legs, and you'll get circulation back."

She did that. I opened up the bag. There was a banana in it, a thermos with coffee.

"I brought something to eat. It's not much, but you won't be here much longer."

"We may not have the kind of money you're asking for. People think we got money, and we do all right, but it's all in the house and the cars."

"You let us worry about that."

I leaned against the wall while she ate. Even blindfolded, she was careful as she peeled the banana, as if she might be doing it in front of the queen of England. She had to drink straight from the thermos because there was no cup with it. She even did that delicately.

When she finished, I took the peel and the thermos from her. "I'll bring you something better later."

"Why are you doing this?"

"Honey, it's just the money. We get that, you go home."

"That box, it's horrible."

"You'll be all right."

"Please don't put me back in that box."

"Not right away. I think you ought to walk around some more."

"You'll have to help me again. My hands and arms are okay, but my legs feel numb."

I went over and helped her up and walked her around the shed with my arm around her waist, her arm thrown over my shoulder. Even having been in that box all night, she had a nice smell about her.

We were walking still when Nancy came in, wearing her mask, hat, and gloves.

"Dancing?"

"Her legs are numb." I walked her around a little more, then sat her down in the chair.

"Put her back in the box."

"There's no rush. Leave her out a bit. She hasn't been to the bathroom yet. I'll watch her."

"I bet."

"Then you watch her."

We both watched her, brought her up to the house, and Nancy helped her go to the bathroom. We let her set at the kitchen table with a glass of water.

"Don't even try to look under that mask," Nancy said.

"No, ma'am. I won't."

I guess Julie was out of the box a couple hours, and then we had to put her back in. She went to it wailing, and it killed me to tie her down again and seal her up.

After that, we took off our disguises and gloves and went to the house.

"It's best to leave her in the box," Nancy said.

"She'll lose circulation, tied up like that. Got to have her out more. I think two hours and a short night is all she can stand. We got to have a body to deliver."

Nancy and I were standing at the sink, near the coffeepot. I had already drunk so much coffee, my stomach was churning. My head felt as if it were stuffed with cotton.

"I mailed the letter," Nancy said. "They should have it tomorrow at the latest. I was just a few minutes ahead of mail pickup."

"I'm having second thoughts. Maybe we ought to let her go and forget the whole thing."

"We'll let her go after we get the money."

(53)

Monday morning, I drove Nancy's car over to a phone booth at a filling station on the far side of town, bought some gas, and made the call.

The phone rang once and a man answered.

I held a handkerchief to my mouth, talked through it. "Rose?"

"Yes."

"We're the ones."

"Heavens, don't hurt her."

"She's fine. Let's make this simple. We need fifty thousand dollars and you get your daughter back."

"Fifty thousand?"

"I think I said it clearly."

"I don't have that kind of money. I'm an insurance agent. The company has money."

"Then they can pay it."

"They won't. Even I don't have insurance for this sort of thing."

"That's not good for your kid."

"I'll give you everything my wife and I own, but don't hurt her."

"Fifty thousand."

"I might be able to get that if I have time. But I don't have that handy. I can't sell my house and cars that fast. I got maybe thirty thousand in the bank. Our life savings."

"That's it?"

"That's it. I do fine, but it's all tied up. I'm living over my head slightly."

"Would you lie to me, Mr. Rose?"

"With you having my daughter, not even a little bit."

"You get that thirty thousand. Make sure the bills are not in sequence. You know what I mean. And you put it in twenties and pack it in a suitcase. Might take two suitcases. You get the suitcases and you drive out to Evangeline Road, and you pull over close to where they have the boat ramp. Right before it is a hill. You toss the case or cases, whatever it takes, down the hill. Don't bring cops, because I won't have Julie with me."

"Then how will I know you'll let her go?"

"You won't, but if I'm not back in a short time, my partner will kill her. Do you understand?"

"Completely. I'll do as you say. No police."

"Best not. We'll let her go within a couple of hours of receiving the money. Hear?"

"Yes. When?"

"Make it tonight at nine on the dot. No cops. You hear? No cops. And be home until eight p.m. We might change up things and call you then to let you know."

"Please don't hurt my little girl."

"She'll be fine."

(54)

There's a lake outside of town, and it's off Evangeline Road. There's a boat dock down from it, and the water out there is deep and clear.

I was thinking about it, about picking up the money there. Our plan was for me to hide and grab it, run to where the car was parked, Nancy at the wheel. We could loop around some trees and take a back road that would come out near the drive-in.

I thought on that, and for me, the pickup was the weakest part of our plan.

I was out in the shed with Julie, giving her a sandwich and a Coke, considering all that. I was watching Julie eat, little delicate bites. I was thinking about Frank's motorboat, about how to change plans.

I let Julie stay out of the box for a couple of hours, brought her up to the house so Nancy could take her to the bathroom.

Covered in sweat, trembling, weak in the knees, she was still a teenage beauty. I think I had some bad thoughts about her at first, but now I was thinking about how much she reminded me of my sister, not in appearance, but being young and all. I had yet to give Melinda the fake birth certificate. I had to do that. I had to do that soon.

When I put Julie back in the box, I didn't tie her hands and feet. With the setup we had, she wasn't going anywhere. And now I was feeling more like a big brother than a horny old goat.

When I finished there, I went back to the house and told Nancy about my idea. "We take the motorboat and come across the lake, opposite the drop-off. We grab the money, leave by boat, hook it on the car's hitch, and drive it back."

"That could be all right," Nancy said.

"I think we take the girl with us. We let her out on the opposite side if the money is there. Then we're through with her."

"I don't know about that."

"It's not like she's a wildcat. She's pretty passive about the whole thing. This way, we don't have to keep her and worry about something going wrong after that point. We got the money, Rose has the kid. Another thing—we're not getting fifty thousand."

"What?"

"He doesn't have it. We're getting thirty."

"He lied to you."

"Possible, but I don't think so. Believe me, he wants his kid back, and thirty thousand, that's nothing to sneeze at."

"That wasn't our plan."

"Plans change. Longer we mess with this, more likely he's going to bring the cops into it. Hell, maybe he already has. Lover boy went to them, we can bet on that. I told Rose not to bring the cops, but he might, or they might be watching him on account of her boyfriend telling his story."

"You think that, then we don't pick up the money tonight."

"It'll be the same every night. But we mess with Rose a bit. We call him about seven p.m. He'll be at home, I'm sure. My guess is he's already gone to the bank and got the money. We tell him what we want now is for him to drive out and make the drop. We'll make it an hour earlier, and we'll tell him to leave right then as it ought to take him about an hour to get out to the lake. We'll have him park, and instead of tossing the money over the embankment, we'll have him bring the money to the edge of the water, on the dock, and wait for us to come out on the dock and meet him. Then we'll show up with the boat instead, have him toss it to us, let Julie out on the dock, and we're gone."

"It's risky."

"It's all risky, baby."

Nancy thought on the plan. "All right. I'll be glad to get rid of that girl."

"And I'll be glad to have that money."

"*We'll* be glad to have that money."

"Of course. What I meant."

(55)

I went up to the drive-in about six. It was still a while before dark, but it took some time to get things going before the customers came. I saw Walter there.

"Thought you were looking after a sick grandma."

"She's all right now. I can't stay tonight, though."

"That's a shame."

I ignored him. I went into the concession. The pimple-faced girl whose name I could never remember was there.

She was so glad to see me I felt bad about not knowing her name.

"How's your grandmother?"

"Fine. It's still going to be yours and Walter's tonight."

Her face fell. "He makes me kind of nervous."

"He makes everyone kind of nervous. But it's all right. After tonight, I'll be back at it. Thing is, I'm feeling a little under the weather myself. I might have got something from my grandmother. What I'm going to need is for you to make sure things are done right. Popcorn is kept fresh. We don't want a reputation for serving popcorn that tastes like Styrofoam."

She looked like her feelings were hurt. "I always keep it fresh."

"I know you do, but Walter, I'm not so sure about him. I have to depend on you."

That perked her right up. "Okay. Hope you feel better."

"Sure. I'm just going to look at the books before I go."

I went into my room and closed the door. I didn't look at anything. I was thinking about tonight and the boat and the money.

I sat there long enough to get myself together, then started walking up to the house.

That's when I saw a car pull up near the theater. A black man got out. It was Cecil. He leaned on the side of his car and grinned at me. He had on a big hat and a nice blue suit and two-tone shoes.

I knew what this would be about. I'd been wondering what was taking him so long. I walked over to the car, wishing I had my gun or my sap.

When I got up close, I could see he was still banged up from me working him over.

"Hey, brother. Glad to see you. You are the whitest coon I ever did see."

My spine went rigid. He knew. "Okay, Cecil. What do you want?"

"I want what makes the world go around. There's two things do that, least for me. Women and money. And as I always say, you got the money, you got the other."

"You're blackmailing me."

"Only a little bit. Got this nice drive-in and all."

"I just work here."

"Not what I heard. Dash said you and that white girl been sharing the sheets."

"Dash doesn't know shit."

Cecil smiled at me. "He knew a lot after I worked him over some. You see, you surprised me the other night. But now, you want to boogie, I'm ready. It'll come out different. And I brought my own sap." He pulled it out of his pocket. "It's bigger than yours, a little heavier."

"I'll take that away from you and make you eat it."

He kept smiling, put the sap back in his pocket. "Here's the thing, brother. You got to pay me so you can keep walking around in that white skin, going to white places, and going in the front door to boot. You got to pay me, you hear? This is what I'm thinking. Three thousand a month and I don't let on you got that colored blood."

"Are you crazy? Haven't got that kind of money. Like I said, I just work here."

"Like I said, I heard different."

"You're hitting on Dash, he'll tell you whatever you want to know."

"What he told me seemed sincere, especially after I knocked that damn gold tooth out. That thing's worth some money. Everyone over there saw your car and your near-white ass going into his place, and I had to wonder why that was, so, you know, I asked Dash what the deal was, and you know what? He told me he did a birth certificate for you and your sister, and so, curious motherfucker that I am, I asked him why you had him do that. That's when, with a little persuading, he told me about the chocolate drop in the vanilla."

"You're out of your mind. I can't pay three thousand dollars a month to you if I wanted to."

"Well, we can negotiate some. I like a little haggle. But just a little. I mean, you don't have to pay shit, but if you don't, everyone going to know you and your sister are just a couple of niggers, and your mother is a nigger fucker."

I gave it a bit of thought. He wouldn't have liked my thoughts. "I'll pay you ten thousand and we're done. That's it. Not a dime more. I'll give you half up front, the other half in a month."

"Not the plan I had in mind."

"It's the plan you better decide on or I'll take my chances with you in any kind of way you want."

Cecil, still leaning against the car, lifted his head and considered the sky, which was cloudy, and then looked at me and smiled. "That'll do, my man. How about five large now?"

"How about no. I don't walk around with five thousand stuck up my ass, and I don't keep it in a coffee can buried in the backyard neither."

"Now, that is a disappointment. That it's not in the coffee can. The other, that could be messy."

"Week from tonight, an hour or so after the drive-in closes. It'll take me that long to put it together. Make it one a.m. Drive up to the drive-in then, and I'll have the chain down. Come through, park in front of the concession, and I'll give you the money."

"Just show up late by myself and you'll hand me five thousand dollars with a smile? That what you're telling me?"

"It's worth it to me if you'll leave us alone."

"I run out of money, don't have a monthly payment, I could start feeling left out, could talk about our racial relations at any time."

"You could. I'm having to trust you. You offer me a better plan and I'll listen."

"I can think of a better plan for you, but it's not so good for me."

"I'm not going to hurt you."

"You already have. I got this clicking in my jaw."

"You'll be fine, and you'll have the money, and I'll have some peace of mind. But you talk, you don't get the other five thousand, and I'll kill you. You get the other five thousand and you talk, I'll kill you. You try and fuck me over, even if I just think you're thinking about it, I'll kill you."

"That there is fucking confidence, brother."

"Don't call me that."

Cecil grinned big. He loved messing with me. "Ah, now, come on. You got the blood."

"Do we have a deal?"

He went back to considering the cloudy sky again.

Then he opened his car door, stood with one foot in the car. "All right, brother. We got us a deal. Play it straight, now. A week from today."

(56)

I had Julie in a box, a trailer hitch to fasten on Nancy's car, a motorboat to hook to it, and a trip to make across the lake at night, possibly followed by an escape from the police. I had to ensure Melinda and Mom had some money after the ransom was paid, and then I had Cecil to consider and this whole drive-in and cemetery thing to figure out.

And, of course, there was Nancy, who was becoming testier by the day, not to mention Walter, who was beginning to get on my nerves big-time.

Now if it would only rain.

In that moment, I wished I were selling used cars and going home at night to drink and jack off.

As I was walking up to the house, I felt a drop of rain on my face.

Damn me for asking.

(57)

At the allotted time, I got my pistol from the glove box of my Cadillac, put it under my shirt, poked it into my waistband.

In the garage, I hooked up the motorboat. The boat was a light thing and easy to spin around and link up. I took the license plate off the back of it and chunked it aside. I found a rusty file in Frank's toolbox, filed off the little numbers on the trailer that connected it to its source of purchase, checked the outboard motor's gas content. It wasn't full, so I found a can of gas in the garage and topped it off. It wasn't much of a boat, but that was all right. As long as it would get us across the lake and back, it was okay.

I had been thinking that making our getaway dragging a trailer would slow us down, so I had come up with new ideas on how to deal with that. I got the ax off the wall and put it in the boat. I got the frog gig too.

I put on my disguise and gloves and got Julie out of the box just as Nancy came in wearing her disguise. We probably didn't need them, the way Julie was masked up, but it seemed like a good idea.

Nancy brought a Coke and another sandwich.

I steered Julie to the chair. She sat and I took the food from Nancy and gave her the drink and the sandwich.

"How is daddy's girl?" Nancy said.

She was talking to me. I didn't answer that.

"Julie," I said. "Listen up. You're going home tonight."

"Oh, please. Thank you."

"To make this work, you got to not give us any trouble. We're going to take you and trade you for the money."

"Damn good trade in my book," Nancy said. "At least on our end."

"You are going to give me back for real, aren't you? I mean, you're not going to hurt me?"

"You'll be fine, kid," I said. "Just listen to us, do as we say, and everything will click along like clockwork. Okay?"

"Yes. Okay."

We waited until it was about time to go, then we took off our disguises and made sure Julie's mask was on right. I drove Nancy's car, pulling the boat hooked to the hitch, out of the garage. Nancy had me put Julie in the trunk.

As we left the property, I glanced in the mirror. I could see the rain-fuzzed drive-in finger of lights poking up into the rain.

I drove along carefully and hoped like hell I wouldn't see any cops, just because I felt guilty, not because there was a reason for them to stop me.

Taking some back roads, I made decent time, even in the rain, to the opposite side of the lake than where we needed to be. I backed the car down to a dirt landing that fishermen used, and then I put on my silly disguise and got out and used the crank to lower the boat off the trailer and down to the water's edge.

It was starting to rain harder.

We helped Julie out of the trunk, making sure she hadn't taken off her mask, and she hadn't. I unhitched the trailer and got in the motorboat with Nancy and Julie. I turned on my flashlight and looked at my watch.

"I think we're late," Nancy said. I couldn't help but think she looked ridiculous in that hat and bat mask.

"No," I said. "We're fine."

"We're not across the lake yet."

"I tell you, we're fine."

I had them sit down in the boat, and I used the frog gig to push us farther out from the bank. There was a boat paddle in the bottom of the boat, and I used that to get us a little more out in the water. I put the paddle away and pulled the rope on the motor.

Nothing happened.

"If you forgot to check for gas, I'll fucking kill you, Devil."

"It's got gas."

I pulled three or four more times, and by then I was beginning to get nervous, standing up in the rain in that boat, wearing that mask and hat, pulling at a motor cord that wouldn't start the engine.

Then it caught, died a little, caught on another pull, then rumbled happily. I have never felt so relieved in my life.

I sat down where I could hold the throttle on the motor and started us across the lake. On the far side, I could see above the lake, up on the little ridge. I saw highway lights, and there was a big light out by the dock. Even from that distance, the light falling on the dock boards made it look like a long jaundiced tongue.

The rain was beginning to be a problem. The wind was picking up with it, and the lake was lashing the boat, which was riding up and down like a bucking horse.

Julie got sick, leaned over and puked in the boat; some of it splashed on Nancy's shoes.

"Goddamn it, you little witch."

"I'm sorry," Julie said. "I couldn't help it."

"I ought to put you in the water."

"Leave her alone," I said. "Stay cool."

As we got closer to the other side, I saw a man come walking out on the dock. He was wearing a rain slicker and a hat and had two suitcases. He stopped there and turned his back and looked toward the ridge. That should be Rose. Expecting us where I first said we were coming. He thought we were going to stroll out on the dock and take the suitcases. That's what I had hoped for. I looked hard, but I didn't see anyone else.

The rain was washing Julie's hair down over her mask, but she was smart enough to keep her hands in her lap. She acted as if she might heave again, then didn't.

By the time the man on the dock heard the boat over the wind and the rain and realized we were running without lights, having just the dock light to guide us, we were almost there. He turned and moved to the edge of the dock with the suitcases.

I banked the boat so that it slid in sideways and bumped up against one of the dock supports. I idled the engine, pulled my gun, and pointed it up at the man on the dock. "You might want to drop those suitcases so we can check them over."

"All right," he said.

When she heard the man's voice, Julie turned her head a little, curious-like, and I knew right then that she didn't recognize that voice. It wasn't Rose, but a cop. I didn't even know what Rose looked like, and the guy on the dock had a rain slicker and a hat on and his back to the light, so I couldn't see him very good, but it didn't matter.

"You don't want anything to happen to the kid," I said. "And it will be nice for you if nothing happens to you. I'm a damn good shot."

I wasn't, but I figured it was the way to go.

"It'll be all right," the man said.

"You bet it will," Nancy said.

The man dropped the suitcases, which were larger than I'd expected, into the boat. Nancy opened one. In the rain-smeared light from the dock, I could see a row of bills.

"Look under those bills, make sure it's all money."

She did, and it was. She checked the other suitcase and it was the same.

Nancy closed the cases up.

"All right, here's what's going to happen," I said. "Julie, you stand up, slowly. Don't want to swamp us."

This was a solid precaution. The boat was really jumping in that rain, all those waves.

Julie stood up slowly, staggered a bit, but managed to keep her feet under her.

I didn't stop looking at the man on the dock. He made any kind of move, I wouldn't have any choice but to shoot him. I didn't want to do that. But I figured if he was there, others were close by. Rose had double-crossed us.

"Julie, you turn to your right until I say stop . . . okay, stop. Now you reach up with both hands and lean slightly forward."

When she did that, her hands were touching the dock.

"Help her up," I said to the man, and when he reached out to take her hands, Nancy used the gig in the boat to push us off from the dock, and I geared the motor up and swung us back out to the broader part of the lake and started motoring across.

I looked back once and saw the man pull her up onto the dock. He reached under his coat, and I said, "Lay down."

Nancy dove flat in the boat, and I tried to get as small as I could and still maintain the throttle. A pistol shot slapped the water near us. I had the boat full-throttled now and it was hopping like no-body's business. Another shot sang out across the night and I think it hit somewhere behind us.

I was really pushing that old engine by then, and we were making good time. Even if the cop was able to get back to his car and call in, I doubted they'd be waiting on the opposite side of the lake. I think the boat was a surprise to them.

When we got to the other side, I rode the boat up on the bank a little, and Nancy got out and took the suitcases of money, struggling with them. I tossed the gun onto the sand.

I stood up in the boat and took off that stupid disguise, and Nancy, still wearing hers, said, "What are you doing?"

"What's it look like? I'm taking my clothes off. I'm going to scuttle the boat. Can you unhitch the trailer?"

She nodded that she could. I wadded my clothes around my shoes and tossed them onto the shore, used the gig to push the front of the boat off the sand, and back-motored until I was out a bit, where it was deep, and then I killed the engine. Naked, I took the ax and stood up and swung hard for the bottom of the boat. It took a couple of strikes, but finally I split the bottom, and water came in quick.

I dove over the side, and instantly I thought maybe I had been too damn smart.

The water was nearly impossible to swim in. It kept lifting me up and throwing me around, and once, I went under pretty deep, had to fight with all I had to keep from drowning.

When I made it to the surface, the water leaped and carried me toward the shore. I assisted it by swimming hard. I got to the sand and crawled up on it.

Nancy was standing there in the rain. She had removed the mask but left the hat on. She had the mask in one hand, my pistol in another.

"You got a nice ass, Ed."

"Glad to know it."

I got dressed quickly, grabbed my hat, and put it on, but by then we were both drenched to the bone. Nancy had unhitched the trailer, and together we pushed it out into the water. It glided a bit, dipped, then hung up slightly, but the weight of it and the savage water pulled it loose from the shore. It slid under the waves and disappeared. If they found it, it was just an old trailer without a license plate or any kind of number to identify it.

We got in the car, Nancy behind the wheel this time. She placed the pistol on top of where she had stacked the two suitcases on the seat. I picked it up. I laid it on my knee.

Nancy started laughing. "Goddamn, I thought you were going to drown back there, Ed."

"What would you have done if I had?"

"Why, I would have driven home, of course."

(58)

As we rode along, Nancy's dark mood grew lighter. She would laugh about nothing suddenly, then she'd look at me and smile with those nice white teeth. She was still wearing that stupid Easter hat with the rain-drenched feather.

"Boy, are you going to get some pussy when we get home."

"I can stand that."

"We might fuck on top of all this money. Spread it on the bed and screw on top of it."

"I think it'll be fine in the suitcases."

"We did it."

"Yeah. We did."

"I wasn't sure it was going to happen, but we got it done."

"We did at that."

"Goddamn it."

"I take it you're moderately excited."

She laughed.

We got back to the shed and parked the car, then we took our disguises and put them in the box under the plyboard and plugged the hole with a rag. I took the time to coat some dirt over all of it. If someone was really looking, they could see the rag and might wonder about it, but in the morning, I'd come out and remove the box and fill the whole thing in using the wheelbarrow to move the dirt I had piled up at the back of the shed.

We went up to the house, each of us carrying a suitcase, me with my gun back in my waistband. Nancy actually did dump the contents of the case she was carrying on the bed.

There was a lot of money there.

I sat the case I was carrying on the floor and, following Nancy's lead, started taking my clothes off.

It was a raucous night, and when I woke up late morning with the sun edging between the blinds, Nancy was out of bed, and a twenty-dollar bill was jammed between my butt cheeks.

After removing that, I rolled out of bed and sat on the edge of it. I was thinking we had done all right last night. No one got killed, and we had a lot of money.

I walked over to the blinds and pinched one up and looked out. It was no longer raining. The day was bright.

Nancy was little-girl whistling in the kitchen. I strolled in there naked. She was wearing nothing but an apron and she was frying bacon. As she moved about, her bare butt bounced. Scrambled eggs were already on plates, and the toast popped up when I walked in, as if it had been waiting on me.

She looked at me and smiled. "I like what you're not wearing," she said.

"And I think you have a fashion trend going there."

We were just a couple of big goofy kids with a lot of money and no clothes on.

We sat at the table and ate as we were. When we finished with our breakfast and coffee, we went back to the bedroom, repacked the money, and made love until it was late afternoon.

At that point, I got dressed, went out and put my pistol back in the Cadillac glove box, then walked over to the shed, leaned the plywood sheet against the wall, and struggled the box out of the hole.

I broke the box boards up with a hammer and took the pieces out to the barrel. I put the busted boards inside and got the masks out of the truck, and Nancy brought the hats out. I poured a bit of gasoline from the can from the garage into the barrel and lit it.

A blaze licked up from the barrel as bright and hot as the opening of hell. The stuff inside caught good, and in less than an hour, it was all burned to charcoal and wispy ash.

We hid the suitcases of money in the shed for a reason we were uncertain of. I think the idea of it being in the house somehow seemed less safe.

"If someone decides we might be in on this, they'll look this place over, and they won't have much trouble finding these suitcases," I said.

"No one has any reason to suspect anything."

"Just saying, we got to think like they might, and if they do come snooping around, we don't want to leave anything lying out in the open. Especially two suitcases filled with money."

"I might have an idea for where to put it," she said. "But we'll need to wait until night."

While we were waiting, I drove over to the filling station, put a quarter in the newspaper rack, bought a paper.

When I got back to the house, I opened the paper on the kitchen table, and right there on the front page was Julie. She looked like a drowned rat. A raincoat was tossed over her shoulders, and a thin man with a slick head and an expression like he had passed a kidney stone and was glad of it had his arm around her back. The caption identified him as her father, Esau Rose. It definitely wasn't the man we saw on the dock.

I mentioned that to Nancy. She swiveled the paper around on the table so she could see it, then nodded.

"Yeah. I'm reasonably sure the man on the dock was that cop, McGinty. Built like him. I couldn't tell in all that rain, but I know it wasn't Rose, who, as you can see," she said, tapping her finger on the newspaper, "is a slight man."

I read where Julie said her kidnappers treated her well enough, all things considered, but made her stay in some kind of underground storage with an air vent. She didn't have it exactly right, but she was close. "The man was the nicest. He had a sweet voice. The woman brought me food, but she seemed ill-tempered. I don't know what would have happened to me had it just been her."

I read a little more, didn't see anything that worried me about her being onto us.

Nancy took the paper away from me and read it.

"Bitch," she said. "I treated her just fine. You and your sweet voice."

(59)

When everything seems to be going well, that's when you have to watch for the turd in the punch bowl.

Nancy's plan was simple, but it was a lot of work for me. What I was going to do was dig up the grave where the pony was in the box, crack the lid, and hide the money in there.

The hole where we had Julie wouldn't do. It wasn't deep enough, plus the horse crate wouldn't be expected.

I did it during the night with the porch light giving me a few rays and the big golden finger of the drive-in giving me some more of the same. Still, it wasn't like working in daylight, but the time we had chosen for me to do it was best.

The ground was a little soft from the rain the night before, but let me tell you, digging a hole like that, it's more work than you can imagine, which of course was part of the reason a lot of dead dogs ended up tossed in the woods and why a backhoe was used to dig holes like this one.

By the time I was finishing up, I was exhausted. Walter or Nancy had turned out the drive-in light, so all I had was the weak back-porch glow, some starlight, and the little penlight, which I had stuck into the side of the grave once I got down in it.

That damn grave was deep.

Eventually, I was standing on the crate. I had dug a little space at the end of the crate, so I stepped off there, used the edge of the shovel to pry it open. It was some real work, and when I got the lid off and laid it on its edge in the grave, a stench came out of there like you wouldn't believe. I'd thought it would have lost its reek by then, but that damn sure wasn't the case. It had been contained, and the odor was nauseating.

I pulled the butt end of the penlight out of the grave wall, shone it in the box. Inside there was the dark, flat shape of the horse. Hair had come off the body, and the skin had slipped off of it in places. I could see white fragments of bone poking out here and there, like busted chopsticks sticking through paper.

I pushed the penlight back into the side of the grave. I had pulled the suitcases down there with me, but before that, I had taken out five thousand and hid it away in my room at the drive-in. I didn't mention it to Nancy.

I stuck the shovel up in the ground, took hold of the cases, and slipped them into the crate. I was about to put the lid on when there was a flashlight beam shining down on me, and a voice said, "That's all right. Leave it open."

The light was bright and I couldn't see but a couple of shadow shapes behind it. I put my hand up, covering the top of my eyes, tried to adjust my vision, and then the light went out and white spots were swimming in front of my eyes.

A moment later my vision cleared up, and I could see who was up there. Right then I felt like the biggest fool that had ever lived.

It was Walter and Nancy.

(60)

Nancy held the turned-off flashlight. Walter had a gun pointed at me. It wasn't a big gun, but I figured it would do the job.

"Look at you, pilgrim," Walter said. "Your damn donkey's in a ditch now, ain't it, tough guy?"

He had a grin so wide, it looked like a row of piano keys.

I laughed a little. Not because I thought anything was funny, but it was either that or start crying.

Even in poor light Nancy looked good, wearing white shorts and a white top, her hair bouncing on her shoulders. I could see the toes of her white tennis shoes poking over the edge of the grave.

She looked like she was ready for a picnic, and I was the lunch.

"Nancy, you are one hell of a con, girl."

"Coming from you," she said, "that makes me proud. But, hey, it wasn't all con. I liked you a lot."

"I don't want to hear it," Walter said.

Nancy's voice was soft and sweet, way she used it in bed. "It's okay, baby. I said like, not love."

I shook my head. I leaned on the shovel. Walter was right. I was a huge donkey's ass, and I knew something else right then. He wasn't her cousin.

I looked up at Walter.

"You're next, Walter. Like me, you're thinking she's your woman, but she's already two or three moves ahead of you. Maybe more. She ought to have her pussy listed as a lethal weapon. She's going to end up having two suitcases filled with money, and you and me, we're both going to end up down here riding on the pony."

"She's not going to kill you. I am."

"Six of one, half a dozen of the other. Watch your back, Walter. Damn, you saw the long game, didn't you, girl?"

"It really isn't anything personal," Nancy said.

"Pretty personal from this end."

Walter squatted down on the side of the grave and pointed the gun right at me. He was enjoying this, not wanting to end it too quickly. This and the money were his big payoff. When I was done for and the money was buried with me and that stinking horse, they could sit quietly for a while, then come back and dig up the money at a later date and move on. If idiots came in colors, I'd be all of them.

"How long you been in on this, Walter?"

"Nancy figured early on you could do some things needed to be done. Nancy used to do a little work for me in Dallas, and along came Frank. Just another john, big and dumb, and we started looking to the future. Drive-in, cemetery, it all looked great to us. She married him for the pot of gold. Looked good to you too, didn't it?"

"Turns out it's not much of a pot. Drive-in doesn't really make much money, and I haven't buried a dead dog yet."

"Adjustments here and there," Walter said. "That's what life's about. In fact, I'm just about to adjust you."

I saw that Nancy was crying a little. I could tell by the way her body was heaving. That's when she put a quick foot to Walter's back. Way he was squatting there with the pistol dangling in his hand, it didn't take much for him to tumble in.

His body slammed against mine, and then me and him were struggling for the gun. I hit him a couple times. We managed to jar the light out of the grave wall and it fell into the crate. I hit him with a straight shot while I used my other hand to hold his gun hand at bay. I knocked him on his back and onto the rotting pony. I scuttled on top of him and started hammering.

Out of the corner of my eye I saw the shovel I had stuck in the dirt being pulled up. Next thing I knew, I took a whack to the back, close to my neck. The goddamn bitch wanted us both done for.

That's when I bent Walter's wrist and the gun went off. Walter made a sound like someone coughing a dry pea out of his throat and then he wasn't struggling anymore. The gun fell from his hand, clattered into the box. The shovel came down on me again, but I was hunched over, and the edge of it caught me in the back again, not the head, which I'm sure was the target.

I uncoiled, wheeled, stepped up on the edge of the crate, and grabbed Nancy's ankle as the shovel came down again. It missed me, and I pulled her feet out from under her. I heard her air go as she hit hard on her butt and the shovel slid into the grave.

I dragged her into the crate. She landed on top of Walter. Starlight was in her eyes. The way she looked at me was so pathetic, I almost decided to let everything she had ever done to me go. But I didn't. I hit her hard as I could with my fist.

She made a little barking sound and then she went limp and lay on top of Walter. That crate was so big, I could have buried another pony on top of them and still had room for the lid.

I left the gun in the crate. I left the suitcases. I could dig them up later.

I got hold of the lid and pulled it in place. The nails were no longer serviceable, and there were no clasps or clamps on the box.

When I had that done, I picked up the shovel, stood on top of the box, stretched the shovel across the grave, and used it like a chinning bar. I pulled my knees up, started to swing myself, and finally twisted and threw my feet out of the grave, then inched the rest of me along the length of the shovel and was able to manage myself out of the hole.

I was breathing pretty hard, but I started covering the grave right away. When I had about a foot of dirt on the lid of the crate, I saw the dirt move. I saw a sliver of light, probably from my penlight.

"Ed. For God's sake, Ed. Let me out. I can hardly breathe. Ed. Let me out. Please."

It was muffled, but I could understand her well enough.

She was pushing at the lid, but the dirt was heavy, so she wasn't making a lot of progress, and now I was shoveling as fast as I could, making her load heavier by the second.

The dirt was still moving as she pushed up from inside. The sliver of light was no longer visible. When I was certain she wouldn't be able to work her way out of there, I leaned over and called into the grave: "There's a gun in there, honey. I was you, I'd feel around for it."

I didn't know if she heard me or not. She didn't say anything back.

It took me a couple of hours, but I got that grave filled. Then I sat down at the side of the grave and wept. I didn't know exactly who I was weeping for, but I knew it wasn't Walter.

No longer shoveling, and with the air quiet and the drive-in long closed for the night, there was just me and the dark and the porch light from the house.

The flashlight Nancy had dropped was on the ground near the grave. I picked it up but didn't turn it on. I didn't really need it.

As I sat there, I could hear a kind of tapping, and it took me a moment to figure out it was Nancy, probably kicking at

the lid. That would be like trying to kick open the door to
Fort Knox.

I listened for a long time, and the sound kept going, and then
it stopped, and there was a long silence. After a while, I heard
something like a firecracker going off under a bucket.

Nancy had heard me, and she'd found the gun.

(61)

That night I slept at my place in the drive-in. Before I went to bed, I took a long shower. I usually used the washing machine up at the house, but tonight I just took off my dirty clothes and laid them in the tub while I showered. When I was done, I scrubbed them using a bar of soap, rinsed them, hung them up to dry.

I went to bed naked, no pajamas, no underwear, just me and my white skin with the black skin inside. I lay there, and now and again I'd drift off, but when I did, I'd hear that damn banging in the grave, Nancy kicking at the lid.

It would have been dead dark down there, and the air, what air there was in that crate, would have been thin and foul and dusty with decaying horse.

Lying there, I felt like it was me that couldn't breathe, and that banging would get so loud, I wasn't able to sleep but in little patches. I got out of bed a couple of times and walked around my little room in the dark.

Without putting on clothes, I went out to the concession stand, made myself some popcorn, and poured a large cup full of soda. I took my time getting everything ready, just like I was getting ready for a showing. I went up the little stretch of stairs to the projector

213

room. Walter usually ran it, and he had all kinds of cigar stubs up there, and the room smelled of tobacco and a little of beer. I realized in that moment that, actually, he had been doing a lot around the place. It made me laugh in a way that sounded like barking.

I don't know why I went up there, but I did. I sat in the comfy chair and ate my popcorn and drank my soda and looked out of the little window so I could see the screen.

I finished eating and drinking, taking my time about it, then I went back to my room, took a long pee, lay down again. Soon as I closed my eyes, I saw Nancy's face, the way she had looked at me right before I slugged her.

Finally, I gave up on sleep. I couldn't quit hearing that knocking.

(62)

I thought about what I should do next, but nothing clever came to me. I went over and visited with my mother and sister a day later. Anything to get my mind off that goddamn horse grave and what was down there with it.

In my mind, I was acting perfectly normal. But Melinda wasn't fooled. Later, leaving Mom in bed to deal with a dry drunk, me and Melinda went into the kitchen so Melinda could fix Mama's lunch.

"She may be dry right now, but she's still drinking," I said.

"It's that man you gave a whipping. He's come around again. I can't stay here when he's here. He looks at me funny, and, well, Mama has him into her room, and when he goes in there, he has liquor. I have to leave so I don't go crazy. The idea of it makes me sick. Him coming here, he's bolder than ever."

"Why didn't you tell me?"

"After what you did to him last time and him still coming around, I thought you might kill him. Or he might kill you. Promise me you won't do anything stupid."

"I'll do my best."

Melinda got a can opener and opened a can of tomato soup,

poured it in a pan, added water, turned on the gas, and set the pan on the stove. She turned and studied me like an insect specimen. "You all right?"

"Sure. I'm good."

"You don't act good."

"What do you mean?"

"You're kind of funny."

"Funny?"

"Off."

"No. I'm good."

"How are things at the drive-in?"

"Never better, but I got some money saved up and I'll be moving on from there. I'm getting you and Mama a nest egg."

"Don't worry about us."

"Like I told you, I have some money, you can go to college and she can dry out. You'll have the birth certificate."

"Anybody ever tell you that you have grandiose plans?"

"I don't see that as a problem. You got to have more faith, little sister."

"I got faith in you, bubba, but not your plans. I been trying not to ask, but what's wrong with your face?"

I was banged up a little from my fight with Walter. Just a few scratches, but I had a story for her. "Fell down the stairs at the drive-in coming out of the projection booth. Set my foot wrong or something. Nothing serious."

Melinda stared at me. She could always see right through me. "This whole giving-us-money, birth-certificate thing, hell, Ed, we'll do all right without all that."

"There's doing all right, then there's really doing all right."

"Whatever you say, Ed."

(63)

I worked at the drive-in, keeping it open, and when the pimple-faced girl asked where Nancy was, I told her I didn't know, hadn't seen her. Like her, I was just showing up, doing my job.

I told her the same for Walter. I was trying to make it look like I didn't know anything and at the same time trying to make it look like they ran off together. I figured them missing over time would suggest that.

For the next day or so I was almost all right. As long as I didn't try and sleep too much, because then I could hear that infernal knocking, hear that muffled gunshot.

I took the tickets, and I even ran the projector, though I had a few snafus. I understood it better in theory than in actuality, but I got the picture on the screen. It was when it came to changing reels that I wasn't so good. After a couple nights of that, I thought I should put an ad in the paper, try and find a projectionist.

Next morning, kind of late, I was out picking up the stuff folks threw out of their car windows onto the lot. Popcorn bags, soda cups, candy boxes, rubbers. It was something that used to make me mad, them doing that, like they couldn't take trash home with them and get rid of it properly, but now I found picking that stuff up, cramming it into a tow sack, doing what used to be one of Walter's jobs, kind of relaxing. It gave me purpose. I wasn't planning on beating anyone with a crowbar or hitting anyone with a rock or kidnapping, shooting, or burying anyone alive.

It was a nice way to sort of meditate.

While I was meditating, I looked up and saw two men walking toward me.

Although I hadn't seen his face that night, way he wore his hat, the size of him, I knew one of them was the cop that had stood on the dock with the suitcases. The other guy was thin and long-faced and lantern-jawed. His suit was too big for him, and it flapped around him like he was a scarecrow in a high wind. He wore a wide-brimmed hat pulled down low over his forehead. I could see as he came up his socks didn't match. One was bright blue with red clock patterns, and one was black.

I felt a sense of panic, but I tucked it inside of me and waited.

When they got up to me, the man from the dock said, "Your name Ed Edwards?"

"It is."

"You work here, right?"

"You can see that."

"Yeah. I can. But we're police. You just answer our questions. I ask you to frog-jump, you say, 'How high, and would you like me to croak?' Got it?"

"Yeah. I got it. But I don't understand what's going on here."

"Only one car here, so I'm assuming that Cadillac is yours."

"It is."

"We're going to be looking through it."

"Yeah?"

"Yeah."

"That's fine," I said.

"What you need to do is close the drive-in for tonight. Put

up a gone-fishing sign or some such, because we're going to be here a bit."

"All right. But shouldn't you be telling the owner this?"

"That's the thing. We can't find the owner. We've called, been up to the house. Know where she is?"

"No. I been running things myself. I mostly do the books, but I haven't seen Nancy around in a while. There's another guy works here, her cousin Walter. I haven't seen him in a while either."

"About the same while as the other?"

"Yeah."

"Here's what you do. We got a warrant to search the house and the drive-in, and like I said, we're going to search your car too. You keep yourself out here while we have a look-see, then we'll talk again."

"Okay."

I wasn't sure they had warrants, but it seemed smart not to bring it up. I had to be dumb about everything.

They went away then, and some more cops showed up, blue suits, and they went to search my car and some of them went into the drive-in concession. I figured Nancy's house was covered up in them too.

I went about picking up trash, but my mind was racing. I was trying to think if I had anything in my room that would incriminate me, and then I remembered the five thousand dollars. It was in a shoebox in the top of my closet.

They looked in the car, they'd find the pistol.

I had legal papers on the pistol. I got it when I worked at the car lot because I stayed late, and sometimes sketchy characters came around.

That was all right. The five thousand, that might require some explanation.

I finished picking up the trash and took it to the dumpster that sat outside the drive-in and poured the contents of the tow sack in it. I did all of this slowly and deliberately.

Back inside the drive-in, I went over to where there was a set of swings for the kids to swing on if they got tired of staying in the car or weren't interested in the movie.

I sat down on a swing and gently pushed myself back and forth. I saw them going through my car.

I don't know how long I was there, but it was a while.

Eventually, the big cop from the dock came out, said to me, "We found a pistol."

"Yeah. I got papers."

"We found those too."

"Good."

"We got some other things to talk about, though."

"Do we?"

"Yeah, we do. We're going to be up to the house awhile, so you stay away from there."

"I don't go up there except for a cup of coffee now and then. Me and Walter. More Walter than me. He's up there a lot."

"How well do you know Walter?"

"Enough to say hello and have a cup of coffee. Enough to know he hasn't been around lately."

I might have said hello to that son of a bitch, but I had never had a cup of coffee with him. It just seemed like a cautious thing to say.

"Here's what I'm thinking," the cop said. "Why don't you come and see us after a while. Just come and talk with us. Some things you might tell us could straighten some shit out."

"Okay. When?"

"No big rush. How about tomorrow afternoon? We aren't through looking here, and I got a bit of stuff to check on.

Come around, say, four or five. We'll be leisurely about it. But show up."

"Glad to do it."

"I'm glad you're glad. My name is McGinty, by the way. Lieutenant McGinty."

"All right, then."

(64)

got a sign painted up on the plywood that had been over the hole
I'd dug for Julie and her crate. I sawed it in half so as to get rid of
the hole I had cut in it with a jigsaw and painted on it CLOSED FOR
REPAIRS. I took it out and put it in front of the drive-in, leaning it
against the chain that ran across the entrance.

I called the pimple-faced girl, whose name was Nell, I'd dis-
covered, as Nancy had written it down in her office, which I now
had the keys to. I told her we had to close for some repairs and she
didn't sound all that disappointed.

I waited in my spot inside the drive-in until it got dark,
and then I got a flashlight and went out and stood in front of
the drive-in and looked around. I didn't turn on the flashlight
because I was looking for cops. It was dead dark out there without the golden finger lit up, and I was glad for that. The cloud
cover was thick too.

After a while, I felt confident they had finished their searches
and gone home. I walked over to the house, went into the shed,
turned on the flashlight, found the shovel, and went out to the
grave. I started digging.

I ended up laying the flashlight on the edge of the horse grave and let that be my light. I dug for hours, and when I got down in the grave, I took the flashlight and shovel with me. I pried the lid off the crate with the shovel, and the stink jumped out at me, but there was mixed with it a hint of Nancy's perfume. I shone the flashlight into the grave. I was shocked by Nancy's face. It was discolored and her mouth was spread wide and her teeth were showing in a kind of angry grin. Her face was lopsided from the bullet passing through the side of her head. There were already worms in her eyes and crawling around the nose and mouth. She had lost her sex appeal. I could see a bit of Walter underneath her, and pieces of the horse.

I braced myself, held the light with one hand and took hold of her legs with the other, and rolled her enough I could reach one of the suitcases. When I got that, I rolled her the other way so I could reach the other.

As I used one hand to put the lid back on the crate, in the flashlight beam I could see where Nancy had dug her fingernails into the side of it, trying to dig her way out. There was blood in the scrapes.

I felt a shiver go up my spine. I took a deep breath, worked the lid into place. I stuck the pistol in my waistband, and after I tossed the flashlight out of the grave, I used the shovel to do my chinning-and-flipping trick again and swung myself out of there.

I spent a lot of time covering the grave up. The cloudy skies let loose with rain, and I stood there and let it make me wet, as if I were baptizing myself of the whole business.

I carried the suitcases to my car and opened up the trunk. Since the cops had already searched it, I took a chance. I pulled out the spare and put the suitcases there, then rolled the spare inside the concession, put it in Nancy's office.

I put Walter's pistol in the glove box. They had taken mine. I put Melinda's birth certificate in there too. I took a shower and went to bed.

The only thing I dreamed about that night was the money.

(65)

In the police station, they took me to a stuffy room with a desk and Lieutenant McGinty. The light in the room was poor, and McGinty looked tired and maybe a little like he had bitten into a sour persimmon.

The tall cop with the too-big suit was in there too, as were two blue suits with their cop caps on.

"Thanks for coming in," McGinty said. "You like some coffee?"

"That would be nice."

"Jeff, get Mr. Edwards some coffee."

Jeff was one of the blue suits. "Sure. You want sugar, some Dow Cow in that?"

"Black is fine."

"It's strong," McGinty said.

"It's fine."

The blue suit left the room.

"I got a few questions for you."

"Ask away."

"First off, you got some scratches on your face. How'd you get them?"

"Cutting brush behind the drive-in, repairing a break in the tin back there."

"Got to be careful around that tin, don't you?"

"Really careful."

"So, what I'm finding out about this Walter and Nancy is that they both got sheets."

"Sheets?"

"A list of offenses."

"Oh. Like what?"

"Before she was Nancy Craig, she had another last name, and when she was wearing that last name, she got picked up for prostitution a few times in Dallas."

"Really?"

Of course, by that point, with Walter saying Nancy used to work for him and having called Frank another john, I already had my suspicions about that. I just hadn't known I had them, but now, it all started to come together.

"Oh yeah. Common streetwalker, sucking dick in alleys, humping johns in cars. Figure that's how she met Frank. He tells her some big-ass story about his property and so on, and she decides that sounds nice. Then she brings Walter in as her cousin, gets Frank to sign a big insurance policy. For a horny man, that ass can do more damage than a grenade."

"You're talking about her cousin Walter?"

"He's not a cousin. What he is, is her pimp. Or was. You'd think she got married and decided to go straight, help her husband handle a business, live a simple life, but this Walter, he came along with her, so they always had plans of some sort."

"I thought their relationship seemed a little odd."

"How's that?"

"Way they acted around each other."

"How did they act?"

"Like they had some kind of relationship other than cousins. Listen, Lieutenant, I don't want to do guesswork here, cast a bad light on folks I don't really know well. I'm just saying."

Jeff came in with my coffee. It was in a mug that looked a bit suspicious, like it might have been wiped out with a rag instead of washed, but I picked it up and sipped.

The coffee was strong. I could feel my stomach churn.

"You look a little nervous," the man in the too-big suit said.

"Nervous? No. I'm, well, I'm in a police station. Being brought into a police station, it makes you nervous. Just how it is, you done something or not."

"Have you done anything?" the thin man asked.

"No."

"String Bean there, he's a suspicious type," McGinty said. He was talking about the thin cop in the too-big suit.

"Your mother name you String Bean?" I said.

"Nickname," String Bean said. "But that part about me being suspicious, that's accurate."

I was starting to feel a change in the mood of the room. The kind of change you feel when a big electrical storm is about to begin.

"Let me tell you what things look like," McGinty said.

"What things?" I said.

"That's what I'm trying to tell you. I just offered to tell you."

"Sorry. Go ahead."

"Thanks," McGinty said.

"That's good of him, isn't it?" String Bean said.

"I think it's pretty considerate," McGinty said. "What about you fellows?" He looked at the blue suits.

"I think it's pretty damn considerate," Jeff said.

"Yeah, I like a considerate fellow," the other blue suit said.

"Edwards," McGinty said, dropping the Mr. stuff, "what we're thinking is this couple, Nancy and Walter, they were running a scam. You see, Nancy's husband, you know about him?"

"Fishing-trip accident or something. Drowned, I think."

"There was a lot of insurance on him, and he drowned, and she tried to collect, but the company wouldn't pay. They wouldn't pay because it looked like murder, not any kind of accident. Not unless you want to call an accident a thing where a guy beats himself up, like with a club or some such, then drives himself off a bridge. Insurance company, us too, we don't see it as no accident."

I tried to look dumb. "Are you saying someone deliberately hurt him?"

"Damn, you're quick," said String Bean.

"What we're thinking, yeah," McGinty said. "And while we're thinking that, we're thinking something else. We're thinking that when Nancy didn't get the money, the money she and Walter killed for, well, they got vengeful and kidnapped the insurance man's daughter."

"You know about that?" String Bean said.

"I read something in the paper about her being kidnapped."

McGinty nodded. "Pretty much of a coincidence that Nancy's husband gets murdered, and when she doesn't get the money, short time thereafter, the insurance man who wouldn't give her the money, his daughter gets nabbed and a ransom is paid."

"How's that sound to you?" String Bean said.

I shook my head. "I don't know. It's a big jump."

"It is, isn't it," McGinty said. "Insurance man, he's the one had the idea it might be like that. Said he got a bad feeling from Nancy when he wouldn't give her the money. He suspected murder, and it's not a big jump from that to think the kidnapping might be connected."

"I see," I said.

"You know what else we're thinking?"

"What's that?"

McGinty opened his desk drawer and took out the shoebox with the five thousand in it. "We're thinking this money we found in your room in the drive-in picture show might be part of a theft."

I had never checked to see if Rose had actually followed my instructions about the money not being in sequence, but I was going to bet he hadn't taken a chance on us checking the money, finding it wrong, and harming Julie. McGinty was trying to trap me.

"That's my money. I been saving it ever since I worked at a car lot."

"You know what we did? We called around and found you got a bank account. Savings and checking. You got some money in both, but the most money you got is this five thousand and it's in a shoebox."

"I always worry about putting all my eggs in one basket."

"Bet it was rough on an Easter-egg hunt. All those eggs and just one basket."

"Now and then, one of those eggs would go in my coat pocket."

"Damn, that's some funny shit right there," String Bean said.

"Yeah, that's not bad," McGinty said. "Let me tell you some more. You got this big chunk of money, like maybe payoff money."

"For what?"

"Now, that we don't have exactly figured. Do we, String Bean?"

"Nope. That part is a mystery."

"What I've got to do is speculate a little. They need you to do something for them for a big payoff. Something like when they kidnap the girl, you watch after her. And there's this, Edwards. You sold Nancy a car, and then you started coming out to see her. That's what the little girl works at the drive-in said. One that has a face like a peanut patty."

"Nell," String Bean said.

"That's the one. You meet this Nancy, who is quite the looker, I understand, and maybe you're thinking you'd like to float your boat in her harbor. You helped her get a car, we know that too. We saw the books at the car lot you used to work at."

"I sold her a car. I was a car salesman."

"But you ended up with the car you sold them."

"No. The Craigs bought a Caddy from my boss, bless him. He died recently, see, and they didn't make the payments, so he sent me out there to repossess it. Nancy gave me a sob story, said her old man wasn't good to her and wouldn't pay on the car. She said he drank, heavily. I had to take the car anyway. I liked it, bought it for myself, and helped her buy something she could afford."

"Books at that car lot indicate you made a couple payments on that one."

"That's right. I made a deal for her to pay me back directly."

"Or pay you in services."

"Won't kid you, I would have gone for that. She could make Billy Graham pull down his pants and jack off in five o'clock traffic."

McGinty grinned, leaned back in his chair, and made a steeple of his fingers, letting his chest support them. "Okay. Okay. That could be. But then you go to work for her."

"My boss died. I thought of her and the drive-in, so I looked for a job there."

"Wait a minute," McGinty said. "She couldn't pay her bills and you had to help her buy a car, but she's got enough to put you on the payroll? Got to admit, that don't make serious sense. There's some fucked-up reasoning going on there."

"I was desperate, and like I said, yeah, I'd like to have had a piece of that, so I went out there. But I didn't get any ass, I got a job, because with her husband dead, the place was doing better, him not taking all the money, drinking it up. She said she needed a bookkeeper, and I said I could do it."

"And Walter, he's there all along?" String Bean said.

"Yeah, all along. He was there before me, and I got the impression he had been there awhile."

McGinty nodded, took off his hat, and placed it on his desk. "You got that impression, huh? Julie, the girl got kidnapped, she said her male kidnapper treated her nicely, and she told us he had a sweet voice. I think you got a sweet voice, Edwards. Don't you think his voice is sweet, String Bean?"

"Like fucking sugar. You could sweeten a goddamn pie with that voice."

"It's pretty sweet," Jeff said. The other blue suit nodded in agreement.

"Julie, poor kid," McGinty said. "She was terrified. But she also said she saw her kidnapper. On account of that, just to put everyone's mind at rest, we're thinking we could get you to stand in a lineup, let her have a peek. Maybe have you say a few words in that sweet voice you have."

"Sugar sweet," String Bean said.

I knew McGinty was lying. I had been very careful with the mask Julie had on. And I had disguised my voice best I could, talking low and even, which was what Julie was calling sweet. Only way she could have seen anything of my face was if she had X-ray vision.

"I'll do a lineup," I said.

"Know what I'm thinking, Edwards?" McGinty said. "I'm thinking you're a lying sack of shit."

"Anyone can think what they want," I said.

"That's right, that's right. I'm thinking too there's a lot more going on here than I know. But I want to know. I'm that kind of guy. I get something on my mind, have a hard time getting it off. Sticks like glue. I got to know what's up. It's like when my wife is putting together a puzzle. She pours all the pieces on the table, and I can't tell for shit what that puzzle is going to look like. She starts to messing with it, and pretty soon, even though there are a bunch of pieces not put in place, I can see what it's going to be. An old house surrounded by trees, a river, a dog in the yard, or some such. And you, Edwards, you're one of those pieces that's missing, but I can see the rest of the picture. You do fit in the puzzle somewhere, don't you?"

"Nope."

"Hear that, String Bean, he don't fit?"

"Heard it," String Bean said.

"You know what else?" McGinty said.

I was beginning to feel like the straight man in a knock-knock joke. "What else?"

"Now Walter and Nancy are gone. Hit the road, maybe, or could be there's this other partner, and that would be you, Edwards, and let's say that other partner decided a third of a share, if it was that much, wasn't as good as the whole thing."

"I wish I could help you, Lieutenant. Really, I do. But I swear to you, I just work at the drive-in. About this other stuff, Walter and Nancy, insurance scams, murder, kidnapping, and the like, I'm way out of the loop on that."

"Guess I'm not asking the right questions, not phrasing it the right way. String Bean and the boys here, they know how to interrogate more articulately. I've just had high school, you know. String Bean has an associate's degree in animal husbandry. And them two boys, both of them, they been to barber college. Right, boys?"

The blue suit whose name I didn't know said, "Ask me to give you a little man number one, and I can cut your hair so pretty, shave you so close, you'll want to fuck yourself and pay for it."

"That's education for you," McGinty said. He sat forward in his chair, put his elbows on the desk, rested his chin in his hands. "String Bean, boys? Will you take Edwards here down to the suite, make him comfortable, ask him a few more questions? Simple questions, simple answers. Nothing to put him out too much. Maybe get him some more coffee, a little massage, perhaps."

"Sure," String Bean said.

String Bean and the cops crowded in close to me. I knew to stand up. String Bean put a hand on my shoulder. I was surprised at how big it was.

"We got to do a little walking," String Bean said.

(66)

String Bean said, "Jeff, get the door. I'll catch up. I got to get something."

Jeff opened it, and we left the office.

I could see a stairway across the hall, and that's where we went. When we got to the stairway, Jeff and the other blue suit took hold of my arms and we stopped.

It was a short drop from the stairs to a landing, and then the stairs turned left and went down into an ill-lit area. Only thing missing was a sign above the stairs that read ABANDON ALL HOPE.

Jeff and the other cop let go of my arms.

"Thing you got to watch," Jeff said, "is that first step. It's a motherfucker."

That's when I was hit in the back of the head and went tumbling down the stairs.

It wasn't a long drop, but I tell you, it hurt like hell. Next thing I knew, I was lying on the landing trying to get up. The cops came down to help me up. String Bean was behind them, almost skipping down the stairs, carrying a heavy phone book, which was what he had used to hit me in the back of the head, I reckoned.

The cops grabbed me again, helped me up, and practically pulled me down the turn of stairs. It was a longer run of steps and a flickering orange light at the bottom made me feel like I was on my way to an uncomfortable place. I didn't need to be psychic to know that.

At the bottom on each side there was a row of cells. They were small cells, and most of them were empty. The lights along the corridor were sparse and some of them were out, and the ones that worked were struggling.

There was an open cell at the end on the right, and they put me in there. The cell across the way had a big black man in it. He was banged up, sitting on a sagging cot near a rimless commode. He turned his head and looked at me, then looked away.

The cops pushed me inside, came in with me. String Bean and his phone book followed.

"We know you been feeding us a line of shit. We're thinking maybe a more personal kind of discussion might give us what we want."

"This is crazy," I said. "I don't know anything."

I knew they were guessing, but I also knew it was a serious guess, fueled by experience.

The beating was pretty intense. Mostly String Bean hit me in the chest, stomach, and ribs, across the back a few times, couple shots in the kidneys. I almost pissed myself.

This went on for a short time, probably, but it felt like eternity and a day. I ended up on the floor.

String Bean paused to get his wind, and the uniforms both lit cigarettes and smoked.

Jeff said, "Want a cigarette while we talk?"

I didn't answer him. I got up slowly off the floor and sat on the bed.

"Nickle," String Bean called to the man in the cell across the way. "Want to come over here and cornhole some white ass? We got you some."

"Nah, sir. I'm just all right where I am."

"Free," String Bean.

"Nah, sir. I'm all right where I am."

I figured that poor man had been through what I was going through, though they had done more than just work him over in the body. They had also done a pretty good number on his face.

"How'd you get scratched up on your face, Edwards?" String Bean asked.

"I was killing a cat and it scratched me."

"You think this is a time to be funny?"

I was in so much pain and so worn out by then, I almost told him I'd been fighting with Walter in a pony's grave. "I was replacing some tin at the back of the drive-in. Walter was helping me. Brush on the other side of the fence was pushing up against it. I tried cutting it, got tangled in it, and the limbs scratched me, tin too."

"There better be some cut brush at the back of that drive-in."

"There is."

I had never cut brush around the drive-in, but I knew Walter had, and I had helped replace the tin. It seemed like a good enough reason to be scratched up.

"Stand him up," String Bean said, and when they did, I braced myself for more of that phone book. "Let's take him upstairs, get him a black coffee."

"You know what?" I said. "Put some sugar in it this time, some of that creamer."

"Yeah," Jeff said. "That's some nasty shit when you take it straight, ain't it?"

(67)

They took me back upstairs, practically had to carry me to get me up them, and then they took me into McGinty's office, put me back in a chair, and closed the door.

"I heard you had a little fall," McGinty said.

"News travels fast," I said.

"Don't it?"

"Yeah," String Bean said. "Edwards here, he slipped on a banana peel. Figure that nigger monkey Nickle dropped it on his way down and Edwards stepped on it."

"You feel like telling me anything new?" McGinty said.

"No, but I'm thinking that coffee, fixed how I asked for it, would be good, Jeff."

Jeff laughed a little. He actually went to get it.

"Listen here, Edwards. There's just too many coincidences and connections going on with you, and I know you're in on some shit."

I shook my head. "Not at all."

McGinty leaned back, said, "When I was in Korea, I seen some bad shit, so there's nothing you can tell me that's going to shock me. You got something to say, something to tell me about, it won't shock me and I won't think the less of you for it. I mean, I'd hate to have you step on another banana peel."

"I was in Korea too," I said. "Like you, I seen stuff."

"You a vet?"

"Said so."

Jeff came in with the coffee, sat it on the desk in front of me so carefully, you would have thought he was serving a filet mignon.

I could see it had some kind of cream in it, but it smelled bad and the cup was still nasty-looking.

"Where were you over there?"

I told him.

"Damn, man. You have seen it."

"Yep."

"Drink your coffee," Jeff said.

"Decided I don't want it."

"That's probably best," the other uniform said.

We stayed like that a long while. It was the first time things were quiet and still enough for me to notice there was a little fan mounted near the top of the ceiling, and it was unenthusiastically beating at the air.

"All you boys leave the room except for Edwards here," McGinty said.

String Bean and the uniforms left the room and closed the door.

McGinty lit a cigar and pulled an ashtray on his desk closer to him. "That Korea, that can mess you up, can't it?"

"Some of the most messed up are still sprayed over the Korean countryside."

McGinty nodded. "Listen here, Edwards. You want to file a complaint about stepping on that banana peel?"

"No."

"That's best. Let me tell you something—I don't think you're clean. Think you're in on this shit one way or another, but you know what? I got nothing. Just a wiggle in the back of my brain. I get that wiggle, I know I'm onto something. Soon as I seen you out there picking up that trash, I got that wiggle. I can't explain it, but when I get that wiggle, I know."

"I don't know from wiggles. But I didn't do a thing."

"The wiggle has never been wrong."

"There's always a first time."

"Who knows, we might see each other again. Want to know why I'm not giving String Bean another round with you? And keep in mind, he really likes that stuff and I don't."

"Yeah, but you know it happens."

"But I don't like to see it. What I said about seeing stuff over there, well, there's things actually bother me, like seeing you take a beating. I don't mind knowing about it, but I don't like to see it."

"You were going to tell me something about why you were letting me go."

"I was, wasn't I? Because you've seen some of the stuff I've seen. Call it a professional courtesy, one vet to the other. But I get that wiggle big-time again, and I find just the smallest bit of evidence gives me reason to prove what I know, we'll be seeing each other again. You can go now."

I got up slowly, because that was the only way I could get up.

"Wait a moment," McGinty said.

He reached in his desk drawer and brought out the shoebox. He opened it. I could see the money inside.

"Guess I got to let this be yours, but I took a little taste for me and the boys just so I don't feel like we wasted our time. Call it a fee for the grand tour."

I didn't argue with him. I didn't ask for my gun back. He put the lid on the box and pushed it across the desk to me. I put it under my arm and started out. It took me more than a little bit of time to get my legs solid under me. When I came out of McGinty's office, String Bean and the two cops were over at the wall near the stairway.

"Come back for another cup of coffee," String Bean said. "Anytime."

I went on out. I had been there longer than I'd thought. It was dark outside.

There was an old colored man sweeping the steps. He looked up at me as I made my way down them. He put his broom down, came over, put an arm around me, and helped me down the steps.

"I see you done had a talk with the man," he said.

"Yeah. We had a little discussion."

"Where your car?"

I told him, and he helped me over there, and I kept the shoebox clamped under my arm. I got to the back of the Caddy and collapsed by the left rear wheel. My legs just wouldn't work anymore.

"Damn, man. You can't drive home."

"Could if I could get up."

"No, you couldn't. Listen, you got someone I could call?"

"Yeah."

"I got to kind of sneak to do it, since colored can't talk on the white people's phones, or I can use the pay phone downstairs. They let colored do that."

"Okay."

"I need some change, and I need a phone number."

Here I was with a shoebox full of money, and I was scrounging in my pocket for some change while leaning against my Cadillac tire. Every time I moved, it was like my insides were being stretched with hot tongs.

"Good news," said the old man, "is they know what they're doing. They didn't break nothing, but they know how to make you feel like hell."

"You say that like a man with education."

"You can say that again."

He took the change and went away.

It seemed a lot of time passed after the old man left me, and twice I tried to get up and just go on, but I couldn't.

(68)

I didn't see the old man again, but eventually a taxi pulled up at the curb, and Melinda got out. She was wearing her usual blue jeans and sweatshirt, and her hair was tied back in a ponytail, but right then she looked finer to me than an angel wearing the threads of the gods.

She saw me right off and came over and leaned down and put her cool hand to my forehead.

"Oh, big brother, what have you done?"

"Me? Shit, I just came up here for a visit so I could look around a jail cell and get beat with a phone book and sent home. Turned out to be more fun than I expected."

"Let me help you up."

She did, and I got hold of the shoebox, and she helped me onto the front passenger side. I gave her the keys. She started the Cadillac up and drove me to the drive-in.

Melinda got the chain unlocked, drove the Cadillac in, parked, helped me into the concession and then into my room. She turned on the light. I put the shoebox on the bed and sat down beside it.

Melinda looked at the shoebox. "You must really like those shoes."

"They travel with me everywhere."

She sat in a chair, crossed her legs, and looked at me. "You've done something."

"Police think I have."

"And why do they?"

"Owner of this drive-in has gone missing."

"You didn't have anything to do with that, did you?"

"Of course not. They're just fishing, but I got a feeling I'm going to be needing a new job. They've closed this place down, and now I got no one to work for or to pay me."

"She run off?"

"Looks that way. Her and the handyman. Could you get me some aspirin?"

I told her where it was, and she brought the aspirin bottle and a glass of water. I took four aspirin and drank some water.

She stood in front of me with her hands on her hips. "So, we going to talk about what you don't want to talk about?"

"Make some coffee, baby sis."

Melinda agreed to make coffee in the concession, and I went into the bathroom and closed the door. I brushed my teeth, took off my clothes, and looked at myself as best I could in the mirror. I had so many bruises on my torso, I looked like a spotted pup.

I took a quick shower, more of a rinse-off, got dry, and dressed again in the same clothes. When I came out of the bathroom, Melinda had put coffee for me on the end table, and she had the lid off the shoebox.

"Those aren't shoes," she said.

"No. They aren't. That's five thousand dollars minus what the cops thought they deserved for wearing out a phone book on me."

"Jesus, Eddie."

"It's okay. I'm feeling better. Look, that money is mine. Why they gave it back to me. They came here and searched things, had me come to the station, gave me a nice cup of coffee and a look at the phone book. Then they sent me home with my money and their best wishes, satisfied I'm pure as the driven snow."

"What are you really doing, Ed? Money like that can't be from savings, kind of work you've done."

"I had some smart stock-market tips and investments. Actually, it's better than you'd think. Take the key, go look in the trunk of the Cadillac, where the spare ought to be. Open the suitcases, leave them there, and come back."

She did that. When she came back, her face was pale. "That's some stock-market tip, Eddie."

"Isn't it? Listen, I should have said when you went out, but I want you to go back and look in the glove box and bring me the pistol in there. I'm sentimental about it."

"Sentimental."

"Yeah."

She went out and got it and brought it back and placed it on the end table next to the alarm clock. She put it there carefully, like it might explode. She placed the birth certificate beside it.

"Sentimental, huh?"

"Yep. Deeply. Melinda, I'm going to ask you to do something, and I don't want any shit. I want you to take the Cadillac, with the money still in it, and go home. Tomorrow, I want you to start moving away from here. College, no college. You get away from here, and you take that money. You can give Mama some, but not much, because she's not going to change. I know that now. She's going to drink it up, but you, you got to go, go anywhere but here, and go fast and far. Promise me that."

"I don't know, Eddie. You're scaring me a little."

"I'm not saying you have to abandon Mama, but there comes a time, if a person hasn't learned a lesson, you can't teach them one. I'm talking about me too."

"That's so much money."

"In those two suitcases there's a better life, or maybe not. That's up to you. Shit. Give it all to charity, you want to. But me, I'm done trying to be a big shot. The harder I try, the deeper I dig myself in. Will you do this? For me? For yourself?"

"I don't know if it's right, Eddie. I don't know I believe you got that from the stock market."

"You don't believe that because you're not stupid, and maybe it is ill-gotten, but you can go on and do something with your life. Just take what's in those suitcases with you. Remember how well you could hide stuff when you were little?"

"Yeah."

"Hide those cases someplace no one can find them until you want to use the money, and except for using some to hit the road, don't go spending it right away. Wait awhile."

Melinda sat and thought about what I had said for a long time. Long enough I drank my coffee and had a sip of water.

"All right, Eddie. I will."

"You don't need to come back and see me, least not soon. Take that birth certificate with you. Now is your time. I mean it."

Melinda stood up. "Okay, Eddie." She came over and kissed me. "You're going to be okay? Don't you need some of the money?"

"No. I'm going to be fine. I got the shoebox."

"Should I lock the chain in place?"

"That's all right."

It took a few false starts before she left, and we both got teary, and she even poured me another cup of coffee I didn't drink. Everyone was always trying to give me coffee. Finally, she picked up the certificate and got out of there. I went to the window by the bed, one that faced the highway, and saw her coast the Caddy onto it.

I looked at my alarm clock. It was nine p.m. and it was one week from the day I'd made my agreement with Cecil.

I took more aspirin, set my alarm for midnight, and lay down. It seemed like it was the next moment when the alarm went off.

I got up slowly, but I was feeling better. I decided on having the cold coffee I hadn't drunk earlier. I washed my face to wake up more, then I stretched a little. It only hurt when I did anything.

I got Walter's gun off the end table and checked to see how many loads were in it. There were four left of the six. One was in Walter and another was in Nancy. I put the pistol in my pants pocket, the grip sticking out, got a light coat and slipped it on. It hid the pistol.

I had a real drink this time, some whiskey I had. It was expensive stuff I'd been saving for an important occasion. This was important enough.

I had a couple of short ones and thought about things for a long while. I looked at the clock. Twelve forty-five.

I picked up the shoebox and went outside. There were a couple of wooden lawn chairs out there next to the concession wall, and I dragged one after me to the entrance of the drive-in. I sat in it with the shoebox in my lap.

I wondered how many people had shown up for the movie tonight and found it closed. I bet Julie and her boyfriend weren't among them. I had a feeling she wouldn't be going out much for a while.

I saw Cecil pulling off the highway, start coasting down the road into the drive-in. I got up and stuffed the shoebox under my arm and moved the chair aside.

This hurt a lot less than it would have a few hours ago.

I walked into the drive-in and stood next to the ticket booth. Standing there, I could see the big finger sign, as I thought of it. The lights weren't on, so it was just a dark shape pointing up into the night.

Cecil drove past me a little bit, got out of his car slowly, warily. He had on a big cream-colored hat and was dressed in a cream suit and wearing those two-tone shoes, brown and white.

"There's my man," he said. "My brother in blood."

"I got your money," I said.

"I expected you would. That was our deal, wasn't it, brother?"

"That was our deal."

He put one hand in his coat pocket, said, "Let me see what you got for me. Shoebox, that's funny."

I gave him the box. He went around the front of his car, stood on the opposite side of the hood, opened the shoebox, and looked inside.

He counted, licking his thumb from time to time to move the bills more easily. He laid the bills on the hood. When he finished counting, he looked at me. "You know it's some short?"

"Yeah."

"That bother you, crawfishing on a deal?"

"Not really."

He put the money back in the shoebox, came around with it under one arm, and, without looking away from me, put the shoebox through his open car window on the driver's seat.

"You don't hold a deal sacred as me. Man's word is his bond."

I laughed a little.

He smiled. "Yeah, you know me, all right, and it ain't much off, but it being a little light, I'm thinking I might have to come back for not only the rest of it but a little bit more. A kind of penalty for not having what we agreed on."

"You're not coming back."

"I don't get to come back, then people going to know a lot about you and your little sissy, my man."

"I don't think they will."

He understood then, and the hand he had in his pocket lifted without coming out of the coat. I threw back the side of my coat and reached the pistol out and fired.

My shot hit the car and then his pocket made a smoking hole, and I felt like I had been punched in the chest. It was hard enough, I sat down.

I shot at him again. This time the shot hit him in the stomach and he bent at the knees and fell back against his car.

He put his hand to where he had been hit. Blood was running through his fingers. "Goddamn, man. You done put a hole in me."

"Lucky shot."

"For you."

"Call us even. I got a hole in me too."

He tried to lift his hand up with the gun inside his coat, but I shot him again. The bullet caught him in the lower jaw, and the bottom of his face came off. His head dipped toward his chest. His feet vibrated a little, then went still.

I sat there on the ground and felt awful. I wasn't sure I could get up, but I did. I could hardly hold the gun, and I decided to drop it on the ground. It was like I'd dropped a thousand pounds. I was having a hard time getting my legs to work, and my hands felt weak. It felt worse than the phone-book beating. It burned inside of me.

By the time I got to the back door, I could just lift my hand. I turned the doorknob and went inside. I leaned against the concession counter. I slipped behind it and got a big roll of rough, brown paper towels, tore a chunk off, and stuck it against the wound. The towels turned dark almost immediately.

In my room I sat at my desk, thinking about the blood I was losing. My glass and the whiskey were there. I poured another shot.

Way I felt, it was like drinking tea.

I eased over to the phone, sat on the bed, and made a call.

(69)

McGinty was nice enough to come in by himself, as I had asked. He saw the blood dripping out of me onto the bed and onto the floor.

He took off his hat. "Bad?"

"Not good. Have a drink. There's another glass somewhere."

"There's a dead man outside and there's a gun on the ground along with your shoebox full of money in the dead man's car."

"Have that drink."

"I'm all right. You call a doctor?"

"No."

"Guess what? You told me what happened, I brought one with me."

He called out, and an older man with a bag came in and looked at me. The doctor said, "It's not as bad as it looks, but he's lost a lot of blood."

"Even I can figure that out, Doc," McGinty said.

"You promised it would be just you," I said.

"Yeah, well, I'm a cop. I lied."

*　　　*　　　*

I was in the hospital for a couple weeks, and by the second week, I was doing a lot better. McGinty came in with a tape recorder, cranked up my bed, and tucked a pillow behind my head.

"Now that I'm feeling better, String Bean coming in with the phone book?" I said.

"That depends on how talkative you are," McGinty said and turned on the recorder.

I told McGinty the whole story except the part about the money. I lied about that. Of course, there was the money in the shoebox, and I told him that was all I got out of it. He said it was four thousand, they had counted it. I knew what that meant. String Bean, the other cops, maybe McGinty himself, had helped themselves to some more. It didn't matter. I told him what I knew except where the real money was. He recorded it all.

At the end of the second week, I wasn't tip-top, but late afternoon, he and String Bean took me out of the hospital and drove me to Nancy's house.

"So you got nigger blood?" String Bean said as we sat in the car by the house.

"I'm part colored," I said.

"That explains some things," String Bean said.

"Leave him alone, String Bean," McGinty said.

"Sure."

"I mean it."

We got out of the car, me moving slow, and went to the animal cemetery. I pointed at the pony's grave, said, "That's where they are."

Jeff and the other uniform I had met at the cop station arrived not long after us and came down to the house where we were waiting

Fifteen minutes later, a truck with a long trailer and a backhoe on it showed up.

McGinty jimmied the back door of Nancy's house, got three chairs out of the kitchen, and put them on the ground by the cemetery fence. Me and him and String Bean sat in them.

They rolled the backhoe off the platform, cranked it up, ran it right over the fence, flattening it, and started digging up the grave. With that backhoe, it didn't take long.

Jeff got down in the grave with a shovel, probably to pry up the lid. "Oh God Almighty, the stink," he said.

The other uniform stuck a hand into the grave and gave Jeff a lift up. Jeff came over to where we sat. He said to McGinty, "That might be her. I guess it is. There's the other man in there too, like he said."

"Okay," McGinty said.

Some more people came out later, and they took the bodies out and carried them off in an ambulance, obviously not in any hurry about it.

"I guess the pony gets to stay," I said. "He's been through some shit."

"All tucked in," McGinty said.

He had walked out earlier to look in the grave while String Bean sat beside me and smoked a cigarette. When he came back, he sat in the chair next to me.

"That part about not knowing where the money is," String Bean said, "I don't know I believe that."

"The five thousand in the shoebox, that's all I got out of the deal, and you and your pals got some of that."

"Man, you shot that nigger good," String Bean said.

"Why don't you go see what's in the shed?" McGinty said to String Bean.

"Why would I do that?"

"Because I told you to."

String Bean got up and headed for the shed, but he didn't go in. He stood out there by it and smoked another cigarette.

"I don't know where it is," I said. "Nancy hid it. Didn't tell me where. She might have told Walter."

"That wouldn't be any better than if she told the pony, would it?"

"She might have buried it somewhere."

"We'll be digging, but I got this feeling we won't find it."

"She was clever," I said.

"You're pretty clever, Edwards, but not clever enough, I guess."

"If Cecil had missed, and I'd got rid of him and his car, I might have got away with it."

"Nothing like that goes to plan, but I think had you wanted to, you could have made up a story about that. I wouldn't have believed it, but I'm surprised you didn't try one on me."

"One thing weighs on the other, and finally it all just gets too heavy."

"You know how this is going to turn out for you, don't you? So you might as well say if you know where it is."

"Would if I did. If I did know, figure you and the boys might want a piece of it."

"That's no way to talk about your local law enforcement."

"I know my chickens."

"By the way, talked to your sister."

I almost held my breath. "How was she?"

"She didn't know anything either. We looked around over there, that little trailer house she shares with your mama. We didn't find anything. Some things were packed, but she said she's going off to school. You know about that?"

"I thought she might."

I was thinking if Melinda hid it, it wasn't going to be found. I was still wondering where my pellet rifle had ended up.

She didn't want me shooting birds. She could hide an elephant behind a sapling.

"Maybe lying runs in the family, though. You left the station the other day, I was starting to think my wiggle was wrong for the first time. I almost felt bad I had String Bean work you over."

"I know I felt bad about it."

McGinty was watching String Bean.

"Bean, he was in Korea too. He lost a brother over there."

"It was tough," I said.

"Bean didn't have any sense or conscience when he left, and he came back with less. Wasn't working on the cops, he'd be rolling drunks. He caught some shrapnel in the head. Why he wears his hat pulled down like that. Never takes it off. Fucks wearing it, shits wearing it, sleeps wearing it. I figure he showers in it. Korea. Some fucking police action that was. They can call it anything they want, but it was war."

"Seemed that way to me."

"I looked up some things about you."

"Figured you would."

"You got some medals in Korea. Killed a gook practically bare-handed, saved some of the boys."

"I wasn't trying to save anybody but me."

"Thing about that shit, you're told it's all noble and brave and heroic, and then you go over there and make it out alive, come back to what you left, and find out the thing you wanted to come back to wasn't there in the first place. And if it was there, you know what happens?"

"What?"

"We look at that good thing and start figuring how to make it nicer because we've seen what isn't nice. Start planning on how to turn enough into more, and more is never enough."

"More better deals," I said.

"Did you love her, Edwards?"

I knew who he was talking about, of course.

"At first it was just lust, then it was love, and then it wasn't. Hell, I don't know. In some kind of way, I still love her. Sometimes I can still hear her scratching at that box."

"That's cold as ice, Edwards."

"It seemed a lot like Korea at the time. I figured it was me or her."

We kept sitting there as it grew darker. More cops came and some convicts wearing traditional convict black-and-white-striped outfits were hauled in. Floodlights were set up and the convicts were given shovels and they started digging up all the graves. Or what they thought were graves. I'd told them the pony was the only thing buried out there other than Nancy and Walter, but they weren't taking my word for it. They were looking to see if more bodies were there, maybe. Certainly they were looking for the money.

"Would you do me a favor, McGinty?"

"I don't owe you any favors."

"This is a little one."

"I'm not pulling your dick for you."

"What I'd like, if you'll do it, is if you'd walk with me over to the drive-in, let me turn on that big light. At night, it's a pretty sight."

"I don't get it, Edwards, but fine. That's all you want, considering what's going to happen to you, all right, we can do that."

We got up and walked over to the drive-in. I wasn't getting around too good, so it took a little time.

"The switch is in the concession."

I went to the door, McGinty following, and pulled it open. It wasn't locked. Behind the concession counter was a little switch, a regular-looking light switch, and I clicked it on. That got the lights on the drive-in symbol going.

"What would you say to some popcorn and a Coke, McGinty?"

"I'd say yes."

"It'll take a little while to get it set up.

"That's all right. They got a lot of holes to dig."

I went behind the concession and started the popcorn popper and got the soda dispensers set up.

Working behind the concession, looking out through the wide glass window at the front, I could see the drive-in screen.

So big. So white. So empty.

When the popcorn was popped, I put some in bags, just like I did for customers, and gave a bag to McGinty. I got cups and opened up the ice machine and scooped ice out of it and into the cups. I decided the machine ought to be turned off so it would quit making ice. I did that.

I asked McGinty what drink he wanted, then poured us up some. As I was handing him his, I said, "You've seen executions?"

"Couple. I prefer to stay home and watch *Gunsmoke*."

"When they throw the switch to the chair, you think it hurts much?"

"I don't know. Those been in the chair didn't have a chance to tell us about it. But figure it don't hurt all that much, and it's quick. They throw the switch, and the devil is showing you your motel room."

"Can we go outside and sit on one of the swings?"

"Why the hell not?"

We went out and I sat in one swing and McGinty in another.

"You thought any more about telling me where the money is?"

"Like I told you, I don't know where it is."

"So that's a no?"

"Yep."

We took our time, ate our popcorn and drank our sodas. From where we sat, you could turn your head and see the big lit-up drive-in finger. Bugs buzzed all around it, like worshippers. The light was really bright where it fell on the lot closest to the concession.

McGinty was looking at that.

"Looks like molten gold is flowing on the ground," he said.

"It's fool's gold, McGinty. Fool's gold."

Joe R. Lansdale is the author of nearly four dozen novels, including *Rusty Puppy*, the Edgar Award–winning *The Bottoms*, *Sunset and Sawdust*, and *Leather Maiden*. He has received eleven Bram Stoker Awards, the American Mystery Award, the British Fantasy Award, and the Grinzane Cavour Prize for Literature. He lives with his family in Nacogdoches, Texas.

About the author

Neil Hegarty grew up in Derry, and was educated at Trinity College Dublin. His first novel *Inch Levels* was shortlisted for the Kerry Group Novel of the Year Award in 2017. Other titles include *Frost: That Was the Life That Was*, a biography of David Frost; and *The Story of Ireland*, which accompanies the BBC television history of Ireland. His essays and short fiction have appeared in the *Dublin Review*, *Stinging Fly* and elsewhere. He lives in Dublin.